DRIFT WOOD

DRIFT WOOD

A Novel

Elizabeth Dutton

Skyhorse Publishing

Copyright © 2014 by Elizabeth Dutton

All Rights Reserved. No part of this book may be reproduced in any manner without the express written consent of the publisher, except in the case of brief excerpts in critical reviews or articles. All inquiries should be addressed to Skyhorse Publishing, 307 West 36th Street, 11th Floor, New York, NY 10018.

Skyhorse Publishing books may be purchased in bulk at special discounts for sales promotion, corporate gifts, fund-raising, or educational purposes. Special editions can also be created to specifications. For details, contact the Special Sales Department, Skyhorse Publishing, 307 West 36th Street, 11th Floor, New York, NY 10018 or info@skyhorsepublishing.com.

Skyhorse® and Skyhorse Publishing® are registered trademarks of Skyhorse Publishing, Inc.®, a Delaware corporation.

Visit our website at www.skyhorsepublishing.com.

10 9 8 7 6 5 4 3 2 1

Library of Congress Cataloging-in-Publication Data is available on file.

Cover photograph by samuelschalch/Source: PHOTOCASE.com
Cover design by Kisscut Design

Print ISBN: 978-1-62914-499-3
Ebook ISBN: 978-1-62914-928-8

Printed in the United States of America

for
Helen Edwina Moreland Nemec
Travis Edwin Nemec
Dennis Joseph Patrick Martin IV

★ *will the circle be unbroken* ★

All my life, my dad traveled the world, entertaining millions of people and financing a very comfortable life for his family back home. Each year brought tens of thousands of miles of potholed roadway, thousands of hours of breathing recycled air while hurtling across the sky and over oceans, countless quick phone calls and souvenirs, and arrivals and departures in the inkiest dark of night. And it wasn't until he died that my father let me go on the road with him—a long, strange trip if there ever was one.

DRIFT
WOOD

CHAPTER ONE

"There is science, logic, reason; there is thought verified by experience. And then there is California."
—Edward Abbey

In life, you need just three things. You need happiness, those moments when you smile and shine and the universe reflects it back. You need love, like when you think your heart will burst into a million flaming pieces because of how good you feel about someone. And lastly, you need a kick-ass song to carry you through it all."

My father used to tell me this. Actually, he said it to people all over the world. Sometimes he would punctuate this statement by spinning around, letting out a screaming howl, and then tossing a scarf in the air. I used to think it was silly, but now I understand it. What he said, not the spinning or the scarf part.

My name is Clementine Jasper and I am an empty soul, or so I sometimes believe. I like to be called Clem. I am twenty-seven years old. I am of average height and weight and perhaps above average intelligence. I have clean teeth and a pretty face. I am unemployed. I have also never had a real job. This is the *big thing* about me. At least, it's what I think is the big thing about me. I went to college and got a degree in American Studies, did my thesis on "Disneyland and the American Dream." I spend a good amount of time thinking of jobs or careers that I would like to have, but they never seem to pan out. Actually, *I* never seem to pan out.

We may as well get this over with now. If my last name rings a bell, it's because my father, Tommy Jasper, is the lead singer of Condor. You've probably slow-danced at someone's wedding to their biggest hit, "Loving Rose," that overplayed, seventies California rock ballad that has surely been the theme of a thousand senior proms. You may have smoked pot and listened to their other hits, or maybe you made out with someone you kind of liked while one of their singles played on the radio. Lately, you probably heard them on a movie soundtrack; either an old song, used to invoke a nostalgia for feather hair clips and cloisonné jewelry, or a new track, written to remind aging baby boomers that sensible rocking out was still within reach. A woman stopped me on the street once and asked if my dad was "the Condor guy." I admitted he was and the woman started telling me, in detail, about how her first child was conceived while the *Barefoot and Broken* album played away on her stereo. I didn't need to know about that—no one does, really—but the woman seemed to need to tell someone. After listening to her for almost half an hour, I thanked her, smiled, and kept walking.

Ah, you say, that explains it. Yes, I am a rich girl. I have a trust fund. I don't necessarily *need* to work. Who wouldn't want that life? I can tell you, though, that being surrounded by people who consider shopping a hobby and brunches to be appointments is somewhat soul-crushing. I really do want to have a calling; a purpose other than to drive from one mocha latte with friends to another. Do something about it? I would, if I knew just what to do. Instead, I find myself endlessly frustrated. Life, for me, is like a lap pool. I have my own lane, but I'm just floating in it. Yes, I sound like an overindulged asshole. I'm not. I am lost.

My sister, Dena, is what some would classify a *serious* environmentalist. She is not. She is the commercial illusion of an environmentalist. She is a "Keep Tahoe Blue" sticker on the back of an SUV, a $55 canvas grocery tote made in a Malaysian sweatshop, a smiling granola-lover unaware of her oversized, clown-shoed carbon footprint. Dena is married to a man who is the assistant director of a non-profit in San Francisco that saves otters or some other noble pursuit. She told me last month that people aren't supposed to flush cat litter down the toilet because there's something in cat pee that kills sea otters. Terrible, isn't it? Dena also has a sweet little environmentally-friendly child named Birch. Yes, everyone pointed out to Dena that Birch is bound to be called "Bitch" by future bullies and classmates, but Dena feels some deep connection to birch trees and always underestimates everyone else's capacity for cruelty. She is really quite happy driving a hybrid car, shopping at Trader Joe's, and planting trees on the weekends.

My brother is named Waylon Simon Jasper. He says his name makes him sound like a sepia-tinted Oklahoma dust bowl farmer, so he has everyone call him Simon. He's an agent. That means he wears exquisite suits and luxurious cologne and is always on his cell phone, and he tends to overestimate the world's capacity for cruelty. He knows a lot of famous people and everyone knows that Tommy Jasper is his father. He represents actors now but started out with musician friends of Dad's. He's supposed to be quite powerful, or at least that's what he says. No one would say it to my face if he wasn't. He's always cheerful when he needs to be and yells at people at the right times. I am nothing like him.

This, you will see, is a story about waking up. It's actually about more than that, as most stories are wont to have many facets. But waking up is a good place to start. It was late May, 10:34 a.m. Pacific Daylight Time. The temperature was in the high 60s and a breeze was coming in off the ocean. I was staring at the ceiling. I did this every morning for about forty-five minutes. Perhaps a little longer. On that particular day, I'd only been awake for about fifteen. Sun filtered through the gauze curtains across the room. I had left the window open a crack at the top and now I could smell the jasmine flowers out in the yard. The vine was one I had planted three summers ago. It grew up and around and over itself until it was just a massive lump of green leaves like cupped hands, twisting stems, and paper-white flowers. The inside of the lump was lousy with tan spiders the size of cherries. I tried to untangle the vine once to see how tall it had really grown, but there were just too many spiders and I kept accidentally breaking the tendrils. So I let it keep wrapping around itself, only three small green ringlets clinging to the fence post I'd intended for it. Back to staring at the ceiling. Somewhere in the distance, a leaf blower screamed in a monotone. Welcome to Southern California.

* * * * *

The night before, I'd had dinner with some friends on the patio of a place on Beverly. I picked at my Salad Niçoise while everyone talked about plans for summer trips and bands that were coming to town. They were all giggly over some secret Miserlou show coming up. I was busy pushing pieces of tuna around my plate. This guy, Georgie, who was with us, noticed my lack of enthusiasm and turned to me.

"Don't you like Miserlou?"

"Sure, yeah," I told him.

"Clem, don't you get excited about anything?" he asked.

"I don't know."

This made everyone laugh, including me, but I'm not sure why. I was telling the truth.

"You have to understand," Georgie said to his cousin, who had flown in from London and was currently sitting next to me sipping a kumquat cocktail, "Clem is a *magnet* for the weird and terribly interesting. But she just doesn't ever give a shit. I don't know what it would take to get Clem really excited about anything. The end of times? Who knows?"

Georgie is an artist with a flair for the dark and dramatic, but he's also kind of right. He looked at me and smiled very sweetly, and his cousin reached over and put his hand on mine.

"I think far too many people have a low excitement threshold, dear. I think you are just fine. Just darling."

Again we all laughed, but it was that hollow laugh of false tickled delight. At least it was for me.

I kept thinking about this the next morning. I did seem to always find myself talking to unusual people or seeing strange things. But they were just things. I didn't need to shout about it all. Did I get excited about anything? Actually, I couldn't remember the last time I was really happy or really sad. I couldn't think of the last time I was really anything, for that matter. I started wondering if I was some sort of sociopath. It wasn't like I didn't feel anything at all. It's more that I never felt extremes of things. As I got dressed and checked my email, I decided that it meant I was just even. I was average. Normal.

I started my day out with a trip to the market for some laundry detergent. The Whole Foods on West Third was its perpetually crowded self, and after waiting ages for a parking space, I was finally able to go in and get some of that lemon verbena-scented stuff I love. They were putting out fresh bread and newly roasted chickens and I could smell the sharp sweetness of the pineapple cubes some guy in an apron had recently cut and set out as samples. Everyone around me pushed carts and carried on conversations on their phones. People with places to go and things to do and people to talk to. I made my way to the aisle with the cleaning supplies. I always loved the smell of all the perfumes from dish soap and laundry detergent and scrubbers and sprays; all those smells coming together should be gross, but they work.

I got in line and mindlessly eavesdropped on the customers ahead of me. A woman was telling her friend about some retreat she went on at a resort in Palm Desert and how the leader really helped her get her spirit aligned with a path to wealth.

"Like, more money?" said the friend.

"Well, yeah. And just wealth in life. Bringing all that goodness and light into your life," said the woman as she pulled a big plastic bottle of water out of her overpriced purse and took a sip.

"Totally," said the friend.

"And we talked about using our lives for good. Like, helping the planet and animals and showing other people the right way to live."

"Sounds amazing."

The woman nodded and swiped her debit card to pay for the soy chips and trail mix.

As soon as the cashier rang up my detergent, I started thinking that I probably should have bought some groceries. Maybe some fruit or something.

From there I went to the car wash where you hang out in a brightly-lit waiting room and watch your car go through the scrubbing tunnel. Your car is pulled through, whipped with giant brushes, and hosed down with what the place promises is auto wax, and then you wait while guys with wet, limp red rags wipe everything down, inside and out. They stand by the car, arms up with the rag still in their fists, to let you know they're done. I am always kind of worried that I won't notice that they've finished my car, that the guy would be stuck standing there waiting for me and thinking I am an asshole. I sometimes worry about things like that, worry that people have the wrong idea about me. My mother said once that she wanted to get me a T-shirt that says *I'm really a very nice person* to wear around, to help me with this cause. I don't think my mother takes me very seriously sometimes.

I sat in the waiting area at the car wash and flipped through a wrinkled magazine, not really looking at the months-old photos of celebrities and the articles screaming about their fashion disasters. I just turned the page every now and again, pausing first to glance at the Muppet orgy of brushes around my car and then to watch out the window as the guys in red polo shirts wiped the dampness from the cars. As soon as that hand clutching the rag went up, I walked quickly out the door and through the lot. I handed the guy a five-dollar bill and smiled, hoping he'd be glad I was so prompt and polite and generous. He just nodded without looking me in the eye and walked away.

With that errand crossed off my list, I decided to try the bookstore next. I was driving down Fairfax to get back to Third when Simon called.

"What are you doing?"

"Going to the bookstore. What are you doing?"

"Working, what do you think? Jesus, Clem."

"What do you want?"

"What's the name of that place in Vegas, with the wine and the glass walls?"

"What?"

"You know, the place where the hostess is always drunk? The place that *my supposedly helpful assistant* can't seem to remember?"

Oh, I got it. I was once again a pawn in Simon's quest to humiliate his assistant. But I really had no idea what place he was talking about.

"You need to chill out."

"So you don't know either? What the fuck is wrong with all you guys? No help. No help at all. Love you."

I didn't know how Simon became this way. He used to be normal. Somewhere inside he still was, and maybe he needed one of those T-shirts Mom suggested too. *I'm really a very nice person.* His, though, would read *I'm not the asshole I want you to think I am.* I pulled up in front of the bookstore and parked the car.

The bookstore on La Brea is my favorite. They carry magazines from all over the world, have a huge travel section, and it's not full of people lounging around on soft chairs and sofas. That's something I don't really like about the chain bookstores. There is something disingenuous about those places where customers were made to feel as if the store just wants you to hang out and read books and drink coffee and be all *Seattle*, like you are sitting in someone's immense, if rather oddly decorated, living room. This is an annoying kind of bullshit. The stores want— *need*—customers to *buy* the books. There is no casual way around that. I just want people to be honest about it. I like to think I want honesty out of people more than anything else. But I hate to admit that the real issue may be that I just don't like weaving my way around people reclined in leather chairs while I try to find a Moroccan cookbook. So I go to the place on La Brea. The owner is named Mar, which I am sure is short for something, and he is young but craggy and wants you to buy the books before you read them. Makes sense to me.

Mar is the one who told me that my dad used to have an apartment just down the street from the shop years and years ago, right about the time he married Mom. Mar said that the Condor song, "Rock La Brea," was written there and is actually about some construction noise that bothered everyone at the time. I nodded like I already knew that, but then I checked with my dad, and it turned out Mar was right. It's weird when strangers know more about my family than I do.

I walked down the aisles, checking out spines of the books in poetry, new fiction, history, humor, and reference. I needed to get a book for my friend Sara. She runs a charity that has something to do with herpes, plays the xylophone, loves ghosts and tarot cards and conspiracies. I guess I shouldn't judge other people's interests when I don't appear to have many of my own. I do have interests. I like talking about intelligent things. I like reading the paper. I like lots of things.

I made my way to the "Occult" section surrounded by books on palm reading and tarot cards. I had to wonder what Sara saw in that, those parlor trick sorts of things. Mysteries revealed and a sense of otherness, I suppose. I picked up a pack of tarot cards that had a Star Trek theme. They were so horrible, I was tempted to get them as a gag gift. But I didn't want to hurt Sara's feelings, so I kept looking. There were other decks, all of them steeped some way in total nerdistry. I just wanted to know what the cards meant. Culturally, each card must have some sort of value. There must be some sort of weird history to them, maybe an interesting pattern to the possibilities presented, the interpretations allowed.

The truth is, I believe in fate. I think fate is a valid and interesting concept. But I don't believe in fate sending messages through playing cards. Wouldn't that be fate showing itself through chance? I tried to work this out, but it made my head hurt. There were plenty of books there on the subject of tarot cards, and I browsed the covers for something interesting, stopping occasionally to watch the dots and dashes of dust float around on the sunlight bars from the skylights. I could see the register from where I was squatting and noticed a girl of about eight asking Mar a question.

"Do you have any books about death sex?" the little girl asked. She had her hands at her sides and was gently brushing her fingertips across the wales of her corduroy pants.

"Uh, death sex?" Mar wanted clarification.

"I didn't stutter. I said *death sex*." The girl looked straight ahead. Mar went from helpful to shocked to irritated, all in an instant.

"I don't even know what that means," said Mar.

There was a buzzing and chirping from my purse, the annoying sounds of my cell phone. I got up and started to rummage through my bag while heading out the door to take the call outside. I hate taking phone calls in public places. I either feel like I am talking too loud and bothering everyone around me, or speaking so low that the person on the phone only hears me as an intermittent low hum. Besides, I was sure it was Simon again, and he hated when I mumbled on the phone.

"Turn the phone off or take it outside!" a now red-faced Mar yelled as I passed him on the way to the door.

I smiled at him, ducked outside, and answered my phone.

"Clem?"

"Hey, Mom. What's up?"

"Clem, honey, you need to come to the house right now. Your father is very ill."

"You went to that dodgy sushi place on Sunset again, didn't you?"

"No, he's really bad. He's in the hospital. I need you to come and drive me there. I've had too many Xanax to drive myself."

"Shit, Mom, I'm on my way."

I looked down and realized that I had a book from the store in my hands. *Fate: The Meaning of the Tarot.* I put the phone in the pocket of my jeans and went back into the store. Mar and the girl were still at it.

"I've got some good Judy Blume books that you might be interested in, they're over there in the back under 'Young Adult.'"

I reached over the girl's head and set the book on the counter, nodding an apology; sorry to have almost walked out with the book, sorry you have to deal with this kid. As I left the store, I heard the little girl's answer to the suggested alternatives.

"Fuck Judy Blume."

CHAPTER TWO

"You haven't lived until you've died in California."

—Mort Sahl

I reached the driveway of my parents' house in Bel Air and turned in with a squeal. I parked the car and jogged toward the front door, my cheap, faded blue flip-flops slapping against the marble floor as I burst into the foyer. When I tried to take my sunglasses off, they caught in my hair. *Nothing's right,* I thought. Mom was sitting in the living room, staring out the room-sized window into the backyard. A gardener snipped at the hedge with long clippers, carefully trimming the leaves and branches. When I was small, I'd begged Mom to make those boxwood hedges into topiaries. I imagined flamingoes and teddy bears and dolphins shaped from the plants. I wanted to tend to the shapes each day, trimming unsightly lumps away with swan-shaped needlepoint scissors. She dismissed the idea as "tacky as all get-out" and informed me that we didn't live in Vegas. *I'll show them*, I thought at the time, *I'll grow up and live in a place surrounded by topiary chickens and lions.* Now I was a grown-up, and I agreed with them.

"C'mon, Mom. Where is he? Cedars?"

My mother slowly reached over and lifted her purse, the leather one the color of English toffee that Dad had purchased for her in Florence, from the end of the sofa. She got up, crossed the room, and walked out the front door without a word. I followed behind her and started the car. She fastened her seatbelt and faced me.

"Yes, he's at Cedars. He had a heart attack. They think he's stable, but they aren't sure."

There was a slight tremble in her voice, in her hands. This made my stomach hurt.

"Were you with him?"

"No, he was at Jerry's house." Mom stared out the window. "I think they were playing ping-pong."

* * * * *

We waited for the elevator to take us to the intensive care unit. The hallway smelled like airline food. A voice croaked from behind.

"Angie, is that you?"

It was my parents' neighbor, Mrs. Horowitz. She was at least ninety years old, but looked like a tight little bindle of muscle, spry as ever. She always used to say that I was the beauty in the family, despite Dena's breezy, model looks. I loved Mrs. Horowitz.

"Did your Dena have another baby? I'm here to see my grandnephew's new baby. He's a big one, that baby . . ."

"No, Mrs. Horowitz," Mom replied, "Tommy had a heart attack."

"Oh, my dear! I am so sorry to hear that. Oh, goodness. That is just terrible. You just never know! I saw him just last week and he looked so fit! I even thought to myself that he had the most striking and attractive calf muscles of any man his age. I love a good set of strong legs on a man. Means he's solid, can carry a heavy load and all that."

The elevator dinged, the doors slid open, and Mom bid Mrs. Horowitz goodbye with a nod and a weak smile.

We walked down the corridor toward the corner private room, and there was Tommy Jasper, propped up in bed, surrounded by nurses. Looking back, that sounds like the setup for bad soft porn or at least a David Lee Roth video. But my dad was barely conscious, and the nurses wore sensible pants and those ugly foam clogs. One nurse was fiddling with the IV drip attached to Dad's arm, another scribbling something on a chart. Tommy Jasper, once a seventies rock god in tight leather pants and excessive turquoise jewelry, was now just an old man in a hospital bed, trying to breathe.

His eyes were barely open and I wasn't sure if he would understand anything I said, if I did decide to speak. He looked terrible; drained of color and wilting. He looked much bonier than he had just days before, as if slowly deflating. Mom pulled up a chair, reached out, and touched his hand.

"Tom, sweetheart. I don't know if you can hear me. But I want you to know that Clem and I are here. I called Dena in San Francisco. She's on her way down. And Simon is on his way, too. He was at the Ivy . . ."

Dad spoke up, "I can hear you just fine. And why the hell should I care if Simon was at the Ivy?"

Mom raised my father's hand and kissed it gently.

"Oh, that's my guy. I knew you were going to be okay."

I found another chair and watched as she stroked Dad's hair, patted his blankets, stroked his hair again. She sat in the chair with both feet flat on the ground, softly tapping out a rhythm on her right foot absentmindedly, like she needed to keep time. It almost made her look impatient, but I knew it was her just trying to stay calm. Twenty minutes later, Simon arrived. He was in another of his bespoke suits, and his appearance in the hospital room brought along the smell of skin creams and sandalwood. He pulled the last chair up next to me and fiddled with his mobile phone. I couldn't stop staring at the enormous watch on his wrist. Huge and gleaming platinum, it looked as if it could double as a weapon.

Suddenly, squeals and alarms sounded from the bank of beige medical equipment. Screens blinked and a blue light on top of a gray box started to flash. My mom looked around, helpless. Dad looked to be sinking, dipping lower into the bed. His head was turned and I was suddenly relieved I couldn't see his face.

"Get somebody, dammit!" Mom yelled.

The nurses from before came jogging in, accompanied by a doctor this time. They shooed the family from the room, and all I could do was stand there in the hall, trying to catch my breath.

* * * * *

We sat in the waiting room, waiting. I wasn't sure what else one could do there. I was not, after all, used to waiting. Simon got up and paced the corridor outside, speaking in hushed tones into his phone, cursing TMZ and double checking that security had been set up around my parents' place. He tugged at his hair as he talked, but it didn't disturb the style, since it was cut to look like he just woke up. If I made effort, my hair was supposed to look effortlessly beachy and sunkissed. Instead, I generally tangled it up into a knot on the back of my head. That was truly effortless. Mom dug through her purse periodically, one of the only habits I share with her. When bored or nervous or uncomfortable, we root through our purses as if they will contain an escape hatch or perhaps supply us with a sudden purpose. Mom produced a tin of rose lip salve and began to massage it into her smile. She looked almost possessed by the power of the lip balm, her lips stretched thin across her teeth in what could have passed for a look of screeching excitement. The stiff and starchy smell of hospital food made me a little queasy and I was desperate for fresh air, but I sat where I was, waiting.

At some point, a doctor came out to tell us that Dad was in surgery. I wasn't really listening. I didn't want to know. I just wanted everything to be okay, to be back in bed, staring at the ceiling. I didn't want to be there anymore.

On May 21, 2003, at 3:37 p.m. Pacific Daylight Time, Doctor Keltner emerged to tell us that my dad didn't make it. Didn't make it out of surgery, didn't make it out of the hospital, didn't make it. Gone. Thomas Bernard Jasper, aged fifty-eight, father of three, loving husband, avid dirty joke teller, my fucking father, was dead.

CHAPTER THREE

"Yesterday's just a memory, tomorrow is never what it's supposed to be."

—Bob Dylan

I stayed in my old room at my parents' house that night, listening down the hall through the evening as my mother cried and made calls to family and friends. I got up in the middle of the night because I heard Mom talking and thought that maybe Simon and Dena were with her and couldn't sleep either. But she was sitting alone in the study, saying *Tommy, don't do this to me* through thick sniffles and sobs. I went to her, put my arms around her, but she didn't even notice I was there. I didn't know what else to do, so I curled up at her feet and cried along with her. I fell asleep right there on the floor and dreamed that Dad was standing outside laughing, flying a kite, and asking me to come with him. The dream was so warm and sun-drenched and felt so real that waking up was just cruel. All that was there when I woke was the empty chair where Mom had been sitting and a sore neck from sleeping weird.

That afternoon, I went with Mom to the funeral home while Dena went to pick up her husband and kid from the airport. We were standing in a room full of empty caskets when my Blackberry buzzed. New email, a breaking news alert from CNN. According to them, Tommy Jasper was dead. I closed the email and turned everything off.

The mortuary was one I used to see all the time on my way to school when I was younger. The front lawn was immaculate and the only indication that it was a place full of dead bodies and not someone's fastidiously charming home was how quiet it looked. I used to wonder if the neighbors ever got scared of the place, scared of living next to someplace so sad. Now I was standing in the middle of it, and I still wondered about the neighbors. I decided that maybe they just didn't think about it. I wouldn't.

I sat in the corner of the room on a wide brocade bench next to a table that was overwhelmed by a giant vase full of sickly sweet lilies. Mom signed some papers and chatted quietly with the undertaker. I had the queasy, dreamlike feeling where nothing sinks in and only the oddest details hook into memory. I tried to think of my last conversation with my father, the last words he heard from me. I thought

I said "hi" at the hospital. And before that? Something mundane; all recent words exchanged with him a blur. I knew it wasn't anything angry but it wasn't anything meaningful or loving either. I pushed the thoughts from my head and stared at the floor.

As I waited, I became transfixed by a small clump of lint and dust that had, until then, escaped detection under the leg of the table. I wanted desperately to bend down and pull the dust bunny from between the leg and the floor but managed to stay put. The funeral director spoke in hushed tones, patting Mom's back and assuring her that Dad's wishes would be followed with the utmost respect. Wish is a beautiful word but it's strange. Isn't it something that usually doesn't happen?

Per Tommy Jasper's wishes, he was cremated. Turned to dust. His ashes were spread off a cliff in Malibu. The day was warm, the sky a clear blue. I worried that the wind would make for an ash-spreading disaster, but the air was oddly still, even right on the shore. Lots of famous people were there; bandmates, other musicians, the occasional film star who was there for Simon. There were friends of mine there too, but I couldn't do more than weakly thank them for coming. Two helicopters laced back and forth in the sky above us like seabirds and were ignored just the same. Everyone milling around looked like flies on a corpse, giant black or mirrored sunglasses covering every single face. I suppose they were there to swarm what was left of my dad, metaphorical flies on the essence of a man. While most of us wore dark suits or dresses, the crowd was sprinkled with those making a statement in bright colors or outrageous costumes: the shirtless man in tie-dye overalls that none of us seemed to know, Dad's friend Rob who wore his white Buddhist monk robes, the lady from the record label in some corseted, crimson crushed velvet number, the freshly rehabbed singer in a neon yellow linen suit. Simon thanked the important people for showing up, told them how much they meant to Tommy. Dena and Birch held big bouquets of marigolds that she brought. She said marigolds were good luck and showed respect for the dead. When the ashes were all gone, she and Mom's sister, Aunt Julia, tossed the flowers into the ocean. The marigolds freckled the water below with specks of gold. Jerry, the guitarist from Condor and Dad's best friend, sat down cross-legged in the dirt, put his head in his hands, and cried. I looked down at him and noticed that everyone's fancy shoes and designer mourning clothes were covered in the fine, dusty sand from the cliff. Jerry cleared his throat and everyone looked down at him in his black jeans, black T-shirt, and black sandals.

"Tommy was the best, man. The best."

Everyone nodded at Jerry's statement and waited for him to continue.

"We've been on this ping-pong jag, you know? I don't know how it started, but we got really into it. Been playing together for weeks, off and on. He showed up at my place looking like normal, you know how he always wore those tan corduroy short shorts and a blue shirt and deck shoes? His uniform, you know?"

Everyone chuckled, but Jerry let out a belly laugh and then continued.

"He walked in and said that he was going to put the ping in the pong. Shit, I have no idea what that meant. I never knew what half the shit he said meant, and I think he didn't either."

More laughter bubbled through the gathered crowd and Jerry, sweet sniffling Jerry, sat on the ground and finished up his story.

"I thought he was messing with me when he went down. I never . . ." Jerry began to sob and people surrounded him, offering hugs and tissues. Marco, Jerry's son, handed him a joint. There was a lull, a moment of stillness, and then another voice spoke up.

"Anybody remember that time Tommy found that huge carnival mask in New Orleans or some place? He kept bringing it out at the most random times, scaring the piss out of people."

"Yeah! That was that tour in '89. We'd set up and turn around and there'd be this giant chicken head with creepy human eyes right up in your face. Startled me every time and Tommy thought it was the funniest thing. I asked him if he used to pull stuff like that on his mamma growing up, but he would just cluck at me. *Bok bok bok!*"

Everyone laughed at the roadies telling stories of Dad's hijinks. I looked out over the rippling waves below and realized that I hadn't ever really heard stories about Dad as a kid. It was like he was born fully formed, long hair and leather pants and jokes and rings and stubble.

After hugging everyone goodbye and hearing more stories about Dad, we all piled into the limo that would take us back to the house in Bel Air. In the car, Simon pulled a handkerchief from his jacket pocket and wiped the dust from his shoes.

When we got back, the house was filled with flower arrangements. The housekeeper was trying to find a place to put them all but Mom told her to have them donated to a hospital or nursing home. The house alone was enough of a memorial to Dad; he was everywhere in it. Aunt Julia busied herself under the pretense of "making snacks" for everyone, but she was really just shuffling in the kitchen, trying to stay out of everyone's grief. Dena's husband, Jake, and little Birch went to the den and watched television. They were transfixed by some strongman competition when I walked by the room, staring blankly at some oiled, muscled freak as he heaved giant stone balls onto platforms over his head.

Dena and I slipped out and sat in the garden. I thought we looked funny, all in black on the green and white striped lounge chairs at the edge of Mom's roses. Out of place. As the sun went down, everything took on a warm glow, as if I hadn't just spilled my dad over a sandy precipice and into the sea. Normally, the sunset would have made me feel giddy, and maybe even happy to be alive. Instead, everything reminded me of Dad. Everything reminded me that I didn't have a dad anymore.

I looked over at Dena, who'd pulled a joint and a lighter from somewhere in her naturally perfect linen shift dress. I didn't see any pockets and, for some reason, this made me laugh, like Dena was some weed magician. Laughing felt good, but I also felt a little guilty about it. Dena lit the joint, took two puffs, and handed it to me.

"Take it, Clem. You need it."

I inhaled a lungful of pearly smoke. The stuff stank beautifully of Humboldt and mosses and fog. I exhaled out toward the iron fence to my left and looked past it to the driveway. We stayed like that, staring off in odd directions for a while.

"Dena, we didn't really get a chance to say goodbye to him. I mean, I was there. I could have."

"No, you couldn't. You can't say goodbye. He's not gone."

Typical Dena. I looked away from her, tried to believe what she said. The sun had almost gone on the horizon and the Malibu lights on the driveway clicked on. I turned back to Dena and motioned toward them.

"We used to draw stories in chalk up and down the driveway, remember? See that little patch near the third light that still looks a little pink? Where the pigment of the red chalk won't wash off? Mom was so mad, but Dad thought it was great."

Dena peered past me to the driveway and nodded.

"Yeah, I remember. We drew islands, big round ones with palm trees and starfish, and we'd hop from one to the other."

"And pretend we were castaways and wave at the planes in the sky for help. Then Simon would turn the hose on us and announce that monsoon season had started."

We both laughed at this.

"Yeah. Simon hasn't been funny like that for a while."

This realization made us both laugh hysterically. The weed may have played a factor in it too, but it was somehow funny thinking about how humorless Simon had become. The more Dena laughed, the more I laughed, until we were practically convulsing.

"I miss this," Dena managed to say between breaths. "I mean it. I miss us hanging out. I wish I wasn't so far away."

"I know. I should visit more."

It wasn't that I forgot about Dena up in San Francisco, it's just that days go by and you don't even realize what you've left out. I didn't even have the excuse of a job, demanding or otherwise. I just didn't realize.

Mom and Simon came around the side of the house, the smell of Dena's monster joint had led them right to us.

"Hey, Mom. Want some?"

Dena held the smoldering half joint out to Mom.

"No thanks, honey."

"Simon?"

She aimed it at him and he just looked at her like she should know better. This sent us back into hysterics. Simon just rolled his eyes.

* * * * *

My father had been dead for almost three weeks when the remaining family went to his attorney's office for the reading of his will. There wasn't much mystery as to how things would be divvied up. I figured Mom would get everything.

We all arrived in our own cars. I had spent the better part of the morning pulling clothes from my closet, tossing them all over the floor of my bedroom. What do you wear to the reading of a will? My father was gone, we were dividing up whatever he left behind, and I was worrying about what to wear. I was particularly sensitive after seeing myself on television mourning for my dad. An entertainment show broadcasted footage of us all on the cliff in Malibu. Julia called me later from the house in Bel Air to tell me in a sweet but pointed way that I looked sloppy on the show. The words Julia used were "a touch jumbled, my dear." Julia, of course, looked luminously bereaved for her brother-in-law. I dug farther into my wardrobe and came up with a sensible gray number that was cut immaculately and always looked very prim on the hanger. I rubbed the material between my fingers, losing myself in the feeling of the weave strumming along my fingerprints. I slipped the skirt on, then the jacket, and looked in the mirror. I still looked sloppy. I started to reach for a pair of heels and then decided a fitting *fuck you* to Julia and her distaste for jumble would be to wear my battered up black ballet flats instead. I flattened the material of the skirt against me with my palms, checked to see that the hem was even, and started out the door.

The lawyer's office was warm and still. We waited in a large seating area while the receptionist sipped some sort of terribly smelly tea from a mug. A small radio on the corner of her desk was playing Bob Dylan's "My Back Pages," and it sounded so soft and far away that I started to relax a little. As the attorney rounded the corner in front of us, the receptionist quickly reached over and switched off the music, a shift in sound that made my back tense up. We said hellos and piled into a conference room that smelled chemical, like new carpet and instant coffee. The table was immense, a polished mahogany color that reflected every pit in the ceiling tiles. Each member of the family sat in one of the padded office chairs that ringed the table. Dena's chair let out a piercing squeal every time she shifted in the seat. The more I tried to ignore it, the more it bothered me.

The lawyer read through the estate papers in a nasal monotone, painfully striving for professional indifference. All the money, property, royalties, stocks, and investments went to Mom. There were three exceptions though. Dena got the Matisse in the study, the one she'd told all her friends in elementary school that she'd painted. This brought a sad smirk to Dena's face and Mom reached over and patted her hand. Simon was left all of the guitars in the studio, the lawyer reading off names and years and serial numbers for what seemed like forever. I could picture the guitars in a case that Simon would have built in his house. They would be lit, like in a museum, and the case would be all glass and endangered wood to match his living room. Simon just nodded as each guitar was catalogued, which struck me as a very adult and masculine reaction. He always knew what to do. And then there was me. The lawyer reached into a brown document folder and produced a bundle of letter-sized envelopes, setting them on the glossy tabletop in front of him.

"And to Clementine Begonia Jasper, my middle child, I leave these letters. They are to be opened in sequence and read initially by only Clementine, the contents therein to be shared with others at her discretion. As you can see, they have been bundled in order and numbered," the lawyer lifted the bundle and tipped it in my direction.

I rose, my chair squealing beneath me, and walked across the nubby gray carpet to the other end of the table and took the bundle from his hand. The envelopes were thick with letters, my father's scrawl numbering the front of each one. A blue rubber band held them together, the color lightening in age to a powdery hue where it folded over the edges of the envelopes. I went back to my chair, set the letters on the table, and burst into tears.

"It's okay, you can have one of the guitars, Clem." Simon looked at me, hoping his offer would have some sort of calming effect.

I choked out a cry and a long thread of clear snot dripped from my nose and onto my prim gray skirt. I mopped at it with a crumpled tissue I'd dug from my purse, patting at the spots where my tears were blooming on the fabric.

"You don't get it," I snapped at Simon. "I don't want the fucking guitar, the letters, anything. I want Dad."

With that, I let loose with my sobs and felt like I was eight years old again. Simon sighed in what I hoped was recognition of his own idiotic suggestion.

The attorney finished his routine, signatures were scrawled on paper, and we made our way to the elevators. Mom held my hand while I stared at the elevator doors, tiny tears jumping from my lower lids and down my face. I wanted all of this to stop, to either go back or be over. I wanted to not feel like a child. I wanted to stop realizing I was farther and farther adrift.

In the parking lot of the building, Mom told us all to come to dinner at the house later in the week. She said it would be nice to all be together while Julia and Dena would still be there. Everyone gave a sad nod and got in their cars. I got into mine and set the letters on the passenger seat. Dad bought me the car for my twenty-fifth birthday. It was a huge black Mercedes, a big, solid, boat of a thing. I remembered the day he brought it over—we drove around the block together, then stopped at Simon's house, and the three of us drove to the beach. It was getting dark but it was warm and we had the sunroof open.

"*This is cool, Dad.*"

"*I know! It's a fucking monster! A land shark! That Rover of yours is pretty sweet but it's falling apart. Happy Birthday, love bug!*"

"*Thanks.*"

"*Is everything okay?*"

"*Yeah, why?*"

"*I don't know, I just sort of feel like I'm more jazzed about this than you are.*"

"*Oh, no, I'm totally excited.*"

"*You and your subtle excitement. I know that you don't think I understand you sometimes, but I do. You are going to be just fine. You'll find your way.*"

"*Yeah, I know.*"

"You're like driftwood, my baby girl. All that tumbling around in the world makes you feel lost, but it's just polishing you up."

I wanted to feel polished up. I wanted to know that I'd find my way. Then Simon piped up from the backseat.

"You know, Dad, that's a really great analogy. Because just like driftwood, Clem has been taken home at some point by most surfers in California."

Dad laughed, tilted his head up at the sky that buzzed past, at all the treetops and dimming clouds and power lines, and said:

"Shut up, Waylon."

I laughed remembering this. It felt good to laugh for my father, instead of crying for him. More appropriate, in any event. I reached over to the passenger seat, picked up the letters, and clutched them to my chest, still laughing and careful not to snot all over them.

CHAPTER FOUR

"The boundaries which divide Life from Death are at best shadowy and vague. Who shall say where the one ends, and where the other begins?"

—Edgar Allan Poe

I got home, changed into my normal uniform of time-softened jeans and a boat-neck tee, tossed the gray suit on a chair, and hoped I'd remember to take it to the dry cleaners soon. In the kitchen, I poured myself a juice glass full of whiskey. I sat at the table, looked out into the backyard, and prepared to open the letters. After three glasses, I still couldn't do it, couldn't hear what Dad wanted to tell me. I was afraid that I'd open the letters and use him all up, that he would be gone all over again. Having those sealed envelopes was like having a piece of him there. I couldn't open them yet. But I could get on the phone, and that's exactly what I did.

I called Sunny. Sunshine Dominguez, whom I had known since I was born, who went to Mountain Ranch Alternative Preschool with me, and with whom I'd been best friends ever since we bonded over a mutual love of the animated Robin Hood movie. I loved Sunny, even if she hadn't seemed to evolve beyond that goofy child. She, like almost everyone else I knew, didn't take things too seriously. This bothered me. I almost felt pity for her, for all the other people in my life who didn't seem to *get it*. I can't really explain what *it* is, but there were times when I kind of felt bad, or maybe irritated, that other people weren't smart enough to see more, want more. That's kind of an asshole thing to say, but you can't deny how complex everything is, and how simple they all want it to be. But I've known Sunny forever, and she knew without asking that the best she could do for me at the funeral was to pat me on the back and walk away. It's those moments when I feel bad about looking down on the people around me. They mean well.

Sunny owns a boutique on Robertson Boulevard called NoWayNoHow that sells small items of clothing for large amounts of money. Her favorite pastime of late is trying to catch the skeletal girls she hires to sell the clothes as they snort coke in the stock room. So far she's caught and fired three of them. It's certainly not that she's opposed to the drug use; it's just a game to pass the time. More than anything, though, she knows that no one miscounts a register or hands out free clothes to their friends like a blonde snowstorm. Sunny, more than anything, likes a good time.

"Sunny," I called, my voice wet.

"Shit, are you drunk? What is it, seven o'clock?" Sunny laughed.

"Aw, c'mon." I put my feet up on an empty chair.

"I was just going to call you. I think it would be good for you to go out and have a good time tonight. There's a party at some house in the hills. Don't worry, it's this side of Ventura. No Valley. You interested?"

I just mumbled, not sure what I wanted to say.

"Of course, the real reason I'm asking you to go is because I don't want to go by myself. But I did go for a grand humanitarian gesture, so you've got to give me that."

"Fine. I'll go." I exhaled and leaned my head against the kitchen wall. An evening out with Sunny could be exhausting.

"Great. That's fucking great. I'll be at your place in forty-five minutes. You better look cute, but not cuter than I do."

And with that, the line went dead.

Sunny appeared at the door an hour later wearing four-inch red heels, tight brown pants, and a frilly powder-pink top that looked like it came from someone's creepy doll collection. I thought about making a joke about the UPS man wanting his pants back but thought that everyone makes those "so-and-so called" cracks these days and kept my mouth shut. I looked at Sunny and found myself a little jealous that I couldn't seem to wear things like that without feeling self-conscious. Sunny had a way of making everyone think that everything she did was the coolest thing ever done. She just didn't care, which is nice, until you realize that everyone else does.

"Oh, I meant to tell you that my dad wants to have all you guys over for lunch or dinner or something," Sunny said as she made her way through the entryway and into the living room. She flopped down on the sofa and made a point of not looking at me.

Sunny's dad was the drummer in Condor and the polar opposite of my dad. Where my family was almost suburban in our existence, Rick Dominguez lived all the rock star clichés with vigor. He has been in more than fourteen car accidents in the last twenty years. He is loud and covered in tattoos of monsters and flowers and fish. He has been to rehab four times; the first two for cocaine, the third time for gambling, and the last time for addiction to alcohol and painkillers. He pissed away a large amount of his Condor money and at times seems to resent that no one else in the band did the same. It wasn't until Sunny mentioned him that I realized the negative effect Dad's death would have on Rick's finances. Sure, there would be a bump in Condor album sales with my dad dying, but there wouldn't be any more soundtrack deals and certainly no more cash-cow tours. Rick was always pestering the management office, always telling them that he should be getting larger royalty checks or jokingly insinuating that they were mishandling funds. Sunny was looking at the books and magazines on the coffee table. I wasn't sure if Sunny knew this was a tense subject when she introduced it or if she figured it out when I did. Still, it was uncomfortable.

"Yeah, that sounds good. I'll tell my mom about it."

Sunny smiled absently and I still couldn't tell if she was testing the waters for her dad or just oblivious.

In the car on the way to the party, I told Sunny about the reading of the will. The story about Simon offering me a guitar made Sunny shake her head and agree that Simon could be completely clueless sometimes. She laughed about the snot all over my skirt, cackling and patting the steering wheel with her palm. She couldn't believe I hadn't opened the letters but acknowledged that if she were in my place, she would probably do the same thing. There's a part of you that wants to know everything, then there's the other part that realizes knowing everything has a cost. Whether it's disappointment or regret or sorrow or nostalgia, there's always a cost.

We wound our way up the narrow streets of Beachwood Canyon, Sunny pulling over to give right-of-way to some cars but not others. I couldn't figure out her standard for deciding who got to pass. I rolled the passenger window down and breathed in the smell of eucalyptus and bay trees. At last, we pulled into a spot behind someone's new Audi and walked up the hill a little more toward a massive house. I had no idea who lived there, but we walked in like it was all too familiar. I guessed it was; I knew most of the people in the house, or at least recognized their faces from similar gatherings in and around LA. Sometimes I think we stay still and the backdrop just rotates behind us.

We walked through to the sitting room, then Sunny disappeared into the kitchen, reemerging with two glasses of red wine. She handed one to me, then took off down some stairs. I figured I was supposed to follow Sunny but instead looked around for a suitable place to make camp, someplace that was comfortable and afforded a good view of the room. Unfortunately, all the seats on the sofas and chairs were taken. I turned to see if the kitchen would offer some sort of safe social harbor but was stopped suddenly when a hand gripped my elbow. I looked around and found a girl of hulking proportions in a flowing batik-print dress staring down at me. The girl had the build of a linebacker and a weathered face that was complimented by the cigarette dangling from her lips.

"You're one of the Jasper kids, right?" The huge girl was staring at my nose, her eyes wide.

"Uh, yeah. I'm sorry, do I know you?"

"I'm Thea. I went to Wildwood Elementary with your sister. You were a couple of years ahead of me." She continued to stare, but now her gaze was boring its way into my earlobe.

"Sure, yeah, Thea. I'll, uh, tell Dena you said hello." The girl just kept staring, her hand still pinching my elbow.

I started to worry the girl was going to throw up on me or maybe body slam me into the Berber carpeting.

"I . . . am . . . so . . . sorry . . ." I knew what was coming next. "*so ... sorry* . . . about your father."

"Well, thank you. That's very kind of you."

For the love of God, Thea, stop staring at me. I wanted to stop time and give the batik monster a lesson on talking to the bereaved without freaking them out. I wanted to tell her to dial down the intensity. I wanted Thea to leave me alone.

"His music meant *sooooo* much to me. Really moved me. You know, it's such a small world. We went to the same school and my dad produced a movie that your dad's band made a song for."

She used her free hand to ash her cigarette into a soda can on a nearby table but never let go of me and never took that freaky stare off my face. She seemed now to be analyzing my left eyebrow.

"Thanks. Thanks, that's really great. It was great seeing you. I actually have to go find a friend of mine. You take care." I ripped my arm away from Thea and walked out into what I thought would be the backyard.

Instead, I found myself on a balcony overlooking a series of terraces, which in turn overlooked the canyon. Some of the partygoers sat idly swinging their legs in a pool, while others stood in small groups chatting and silently sizing each other up. I spotted Sunny standing by a tree talking to some friends. There were tiki torches ringing the walkways and I watched Thea, now suddenly outside, make her way over to one and use it to light a cigarette. I took a sip of wine and leaned against the redwood railing. This was exactly what I was looking for: an observation platform where I could see everyone, hear snippets of conversations, but not have to talk to anyone myself. It was perfect.

I heard footsteps on the deck and turned to see a guy standing beside me.

"Clem, right?" He gave me a sort of half smile.

I recognized him but couldn't place his name. He looked like most guys I met; good-looking, with some of those good looks tied into how dirty he seemed. I really wished sometimes that dirty was cute on girls too. It certainly would save a lot of time. He didn't have the creepy polish of most male LA residents though. His jeans were slouchy and worn, but not in that fake pre-distressed way that makes the wearer look recently dragged by a truck, and it did not appear he waxed his eyebrows. I smiled and half waved, gave a little nod. I noticed his shirt was inside out.

"My name's Casey."

"Nice to meet you."

"Actually, I think we might have met once before. My friend Sam used to go out with Sunny." Then I remembered. We hadn't been introduced, but I remembered listening to him try to explain who Flannery O'Connor was to some moron at the Rainbow, of all places.

"Yeah, that's right."

"I saw Sunny. She told me about your dad. I'm really sorry about that."

"Thanks." I pictured the letters sitting on my kitchen table. I was sorry about it too.

He looked out at the canyon, then pulled a flask out of his back pocket, tipping it my way. "Want some?"

I took a sip, deduced it was vodka of some sort, and handed it back to him. He took a long slug from it and set the flask on the railing.

"So tell me, Clem. What's the worst thing you've ever done?"

I wasn't sure what to say. Who asks something like that?

"Why do you want to know?"

"I'm just making conversation. I think the answer to that question tells a lot about a person."

What a douchebag. He didn't seem like the weird, faux-sensitive type, but maybe I had been wrong. I tried to think of something that sounded terrible but wasn't that bad. I looked down at the rest of the people there, listened to their snippets of normal conversations: *he's producing this crazy folk hip hop album . . . you should tell Mick that the tiki torches are a fire hazard . . . so I stopped going to the restorative meditation classes . . . yeah, thanks, these are my favorite pants.* I should have just bullshitted like everyone else, like I normally do. Instead, for whatever reason, I told the truth.

"Well, when I was about fifteen, there was this girl in my high school that no one really liked. She just didn't seem to fit in, you know? Her hair was never right, and her clothes were always a little off."

I realized that even the beginning of this story was making me look like every other incredible asshole who didn't care about anything more than the superficial and banal.

"Anyway, one day a couple of my friends and I poured gallons of Kool-Aid into her locker and put these leaky baggies of Kool-Aid in her backpack. Everything she had, all her books and stuff, got soaked and stained bright red and everyone was laughing at her. But I immediately felt horrible. It was like I suddenly saw how awful I was and I wanted so badly to just rewind and make it all go away. I remember I went up to her after school and tried to help her clean up her locker and stuff. She looked at me with no emotion, nothing. Just stared at me and then said 'Go away, you rich fucking cunt.' I tried to tell her I was sorry, but she just kept telling me to go away. I wanted to die, you know? It was terrible."

I couldn't believe I'd just told him all that. Casey just stood there silent, looking out over the yard. I began to worry that maybe the girl was his sister or something.

"That's pretty shitty, what you did to that girl. What happened to her?"

"I'm not sure. Maybe she's got the best life ever now. I don't know. I hope so."

I was feeling bad all over again.

"Well, it's kind of fucked up, but it's not murder."

Casey looked at me and then drained the rest of the flask. "The worst thing I've ever done was not bring more booze to this party."

"You're an asshole."

"Okay, okay. The worst thing I've ever done was to beat up some guy in the parking lot of a Dodger game."

Casey looked at me like he hoped that was enough. I just stared back at him, so he continued.

"This was, like, five years ago. I'd just broken up with my girlfriend and was pissed off at everything. She said she needed some time by herself, but then I found out she was already fucking some gross hairdresser guy. I was a mess. Anyway, my friends and I were leaving the game and were right by our car in the lot when some guy walked by laughing. I think I knew that the guy was just laughing at a friend's joke but I wanted to think he was laughing at me. I got in his face and started shouting at him and then just started swinging. I knocked out three of his teeth and my friends were all freaking out, yelling at me to stop. The guy was screaming for his friend but the other dude was long gone, just ran for it. I bolted before stadium security and the cops could catch me. We just got in the car and drove off. My friends were disgusted. I couldn't tell them why I did it, because I didn't really know. I'm not violent like that. Not at all. It wasn't like me, I swear."

I didn't know what to make of that, other than it was grossly aggressive. He kept saying that it wasn't like him and that he wasn't violent. Part of me didn't really care. Violent or not, he was just some guy on a balcony. But there was something kind of tender in his admission that I admired. In a social universe populated by the false, he felt real.

"So what did you learn about me?" Casey asked.

"I don't know," I told him. "I guess everyone does something bad that they regret."

"Sure do."

I stood on the balcony with Casey after that for what I figured was hours, drinking myself silly and pretending that I was one of those people who don't get it, don't care. We talked about his old punk band, people we knew, stupid things we did when we were younger, stupid things we did recently. After a while, Casey ducked inside to use the bathroom and try and find more drinks, now that the flask was empty and back in his pocket. I looked down at the terrace below and saw Sunny. She waved, nodded, then made a crude gesture with her hands. I laughed and shook my head.

"What is she doing?"

Casey was now standing next to me, a bottle of wine in his hand. Sunny stood below us, frozen, then turned away and tripped over a large teak deck chair.

"Was Sunny making the international third graders' sign for fucking?" Casey looked over at me, eyebrows raised.

"Yes, I believe she was."

Casey shrugged, laughed, and took a sip from the bottle.

I was beginning to enjoy it out on the balcony with Casey. It was warm and I was full of booze and everything was turning out to be funny, and I felt, for the first time in a couple of weeks, that I could just exist without trying.

It got later and people started to head out, either to go home or on to some other party at someone's warehouse loft downtown. We moved from the balcony into the living room of the house and then shuffled out the front door with all of Casey's friends and Sunny.

"Well, I guess the party's over," Casey was looking at me with his head cocked to the side. I couldn't tell if this was a suggestion that we go somewhere else. Now that I was up and moving, the alcohol was really starting to hit me and I felt kind of loose and daring. "Yeah, well, we—" I was trying to think of something to say to keep him around a little longer. I wanted to keep forgetting. "We could go to Original Tommy's or something and get a burger. Hit up a taco truck. Something."

"I had fun tonight. See you around, kiddo." And with that, Casey waved and walked off with his friends, piling into some SUV and then driving off into the night.

He just left. Shit, he called me *kiddo*. The word woke me up, made me see that there was no use drifting off into the evening with some jackass, and that my life hadn't changed a bit. Not that I'd expected it to, exactly, but for that time on the balcony I was able to forget about my dad and Condor and the look on Mom's face when we spilled Dad into the air and the ocean.

"Did he call you 'kiddo'?" Sunny asked me as I rested my head against the car window while she drove me home. "What the fuck was that?"

"Yeah, a little dismissive, right?" I looked out the window at the hazy night sky. Twenty minutes ago, I was drunk and hopeful. Now I was drunk and sullen. "Hey, Sunny? What's the worst thing you've ever done?"

Sunny looked at me and then back at the road.

"Shit, that's a long list. Um, I guess the worst thing I ever did was when I was four and set that fire in my mom's garage. No, I know! The worst thing I ever did was take a huge bag of coke from my dad's bedside table. I mean, *holy shit,* it was a monster bag. He flipped out because it was gone and I told my mom that I took it and flushed it because I wanted Dad to get clean. Everyone got all weepy and was, like, 'Rick! You've got to stop . . . even your child is begging you!'" Sunny started laughing. "I hid it in my tree house out back at my mom's and was sniffing on it all summer."

"I never knew about that. How old were you?" I tried to remember Rick's last intervention.

"I don't know. Twelve? Fucked up, huh?"

"Do you regret it?"

"I only regret not taking more of his stuff over the years. Now that he's all healthy guy, the only shit in his house is protein powder and liquid vitamins."

Somehow I doubted that. I waited for Sunny to ask about my worst deed but she just kept driving, giggling every now and then and saying, "Rick! Think about the kid!" I couldn't tell how wasted Sunny was, or if she was drunk at all. She held her substances closely, only revealing altered states at her most extreme. I leaned my head back against the window and watched the reflection of Sunny's car in the dark mirror of closed shop windows. As different as Sunny and I seemed, we'd both lived lives unlike most others and we understood each other. Sunny knew me well and knew it was best to just let me simmer.

Sunny dropped me off at home, complaining about having to do inventory the next morning. I said goodbye and sat on the front steps, looking at the sky. There were no stars, just the fuzzy gray velour of smog and streetlights. Everything was slipping away and I had no power to stop any of it. Everything just seemed empty.

* * * * *

I woke up the next morning feeling terrible and still in the clothes I wore the night before, shoes included. I'd slept on the sofa in the living room but couldn't remember why. As I made my way to the kitchen, I thought about the letters and figured now was as good a time as any. I took a deep breath and sat at the kitchen table, still in last night's clothes but not in last night's frame of mind. I opened Letter One.

Dear Clem,

Hello! Hey there! Testing, one . . . two . . . is this thing on? Ha ha ha! You are reading this letter, so that means I am gone. I am coming at you from the cosmic beyond! I hope you are hanging in there. This is a weird letter to write, you know? I am sitting here in the study, trying to figure out how I can put this all into words, and it's not easy. But there are some things in life that you just gotta do. That's the truth.

I'm telling all of this to you because I think that you are the one in the family who will understand it best. You are also the one in the family who needs this the most. Nothing but good can come of this, Sweetpea, even though I am going to drop some heavy shit your way. But when I tell you that there are some things you have to do, that's the heart of the matter.

Words and music are (shit, if you are reading this, then they WERE) my life. You gotta be able to laugh, Clem. You know that. It's actually pretty wild imagining that I am already dead. Tripping me out. Anyway, the early part of my life as a musician means a lot to me. I built who I was when I was playing shows in small towns and just happy to be out there singing and sharing the stories and the music. There were no agents or managers. There was no merchandise. There was no money. But it was amazing, and it was the foundation for the man I became. It was the foundation of our family as well.

You remember 1985. You remember when I tried to make it on my own, without the band, and express myself in an album that was all me. Those guys are (sorry, were! Ha ha ha) my brothers, and they will always be connected to me in the universe. But I had things to say that came just from me. You also remember how fucking brutal the critics were. I put <u>everything</u> into "Bathtub Epiphany," and no one got it. I admit it wasn't the best record around, but it crushed me, baby, and after that I knew that I needed the other guys in order to communicate with the other human ears and minds on the planet. But out there in the spooky dusty corners of my mind was something else I wanted to share with the world. I wanted to tell my story about the early days and my life in the belly of California.

I traveled all over this great state and she made me a full-grown man. I found myself in California, in the small, piece-of-shit towns and the incredible cities. That's what I want you to do. I want you to go to the places that made me and soak up all the essence, just like I did. I want you to be on the road and see things whirring by and smell disgusting gas station toilets and watch the sun go down over the ocean and feel the dirt in a tomato field and hear the music of it all.

You have to walk that road. You observe people and places like no one else. You see things. (Not like hallucinations, ha ha ha). You have to make some discoveries, my darling. You will learn a lot on the way about me, about you, about California, about life, about family, about how we see other human beings and how other people see us. You may even need to right some wrongs, slay some dragons, and set the cosmos back in order. Who knows?

You know me as Dad. Papa. The guy who cried when you started college, who taught you how to drive a stick shift, who gave you them blue peepers. And you also sort of know me as the guy from Condor. You see the way that the public sees me—some (once) long-haired singer bringing a little bit of escape to people through their radios and in their arenas. But those two Tommys aren't the only Tommys. There's the me that your mom knows. The me that Jerry knows. The me that my manager knows. The me that strangers meet. Every single person on earth is like that, full of the different people that they are to those they come in contact with. The final me, the final Tommy, is the one that I know. It's the one I made. That's the Tommy I try to show everybody. But just like iridescent fabric, those crazy sharkskin suits (I can't think of a better metaphor right now), it is essentially always the same color, but looks like different colors to different people, depending on where they are standing. Does that make sense? We are who we are, but we are also who we are to the receiver, so to speak. You are like that.

Everyone. I am hoping that part of all this, all these letters and my rambling, will be a chance for you to come the closest to understanding my me. I want you to see me from as close to my perspective as possible.

Of course, that may be a little too much to ask of the universe, and I could be pissing up a tree with all this. Just keep it in mind.

Why couldn't we do this when I wasn't dead? I know that's what you're thinking. I am in your mind now and haunting you, baby! It's okay to laugh. I know that your mother won't be happy with the tone of these letters. She would want it to be formal, blah blah blah. I love her more than anything but she's a stick in the mud that way. Back to why now. I can't let my fears and inadequacies taint this for you. I have to be gone. I have to be out of the picture for you to do this. I'll haunt the shit out of you if you decide not to, but that's your choice. But it's what I want for you. You are so adrift in the world sometimes, and I feel like this is the project that the universe has created for you so that you can share your beauty and magic with everyone. I want you to bring peace to things, and that can't happen with me around.

Letter Two will tell you where to start. Each letter after that tells you where to go from there. Don't open them and read them all at once. There will be no mystery then, and it won't be fun. This isn't a yellow brick road or a scavenger hunt. It's a cosmic path I want to share. It's a look inside. It's a big reveal. I want you to be free and to know the love that I know.

I know you love rockin' down the highway and all, but when you are on this trip, don't listen to any Condor, please. I have my reasons.

I love you, Clementine. I love you with all the stars and planets and rainbows and sunshine and flowers and ocean waves in the world.

xoxoxoxoxoxoxoxoxoxo

Dad

P.S.—I was going to sign it "Dearly Departed Dad," but then thought better of it. Smile!

* * * * *

If there was a point, I was missing it. The letter didn't really make any sense, which was tickling a feeling of irritation. I should have expected this. Dad loved the feeling of not knowing, of just letting go into something. Freefalling, so to speak. When I was a kid, I would freak out at the start of every school year. I'd just spent the last year learning all sorts of stuff and paying attention and doing everything right, and now I had to do it all over again but with new materials. This scared the shit out of me. Most years when I was growing up, my father was either on tour or recording or generally not available in person when school started. I would fret and cry until my mother could get him on the phone and he would somehow talk me down. I couldn't remember what he told me—although I did remember that the talk he gave before my first day of high school lasted almost five hours—but he always got me hip to the idea that not knowing what would happen was the best part. It was a lesson I had to relearn over and over. It was a lesson I still hadn't totally absorbed.

* * * * *

I arrived at my mom's house for dinner, the letter tucked into my back pocket. Dena and her eco-family had already gone back to San Francisco, something Mom understood but still grumbled about. Simon got to the house not long after I did, cruising through the front door while talking on his cell phone.

Aunt Julia, still not returned to Dallas, stood in the kitchen with Mom, cutting up cucumber and avocado for the salad. She had her back to the rest of the kitchen, and I was positively mystified by how *huge* Julia's hair was. Dena always described her as "coiffed." It was as if someone asked a police sketch artist to draw an upper-middle-class matron, you'd get a portrait of Julia. Composed. Mom was also always composed but not in that whipped and frosted way. I guessed it was the Dallas vs Los Angeles thing and wondered if my mother would have been more like Julia if she'd never left Texas. They both had steely, solid cores, just different costumes. Julia was a barrage of sorbet-colored sweater sets and big clip earrings, lacquered nails and strong perfume. Mom was all cashmere jogging suits, freckles, and designer sandals. She and Julia had the same ditzy charm that everyone seemed to love, though. They were both easily confused and generally dissolved into giggles when things got tense or too much. They were accessories to their husbands, their families.

Window dressing. Don't get me wrong, I love my mother. I just realized the reality of the situation.

Neither one would accept my halfhearted offer of help, so I sat at the little breakfast table by the French doors that lead out to the patio. The doors were open and I could tell the gardener had been by that day because the patio bricks had been recently hosed down and were wet and deep red, like inside a lip. I could smell the fresh-cut grass from the lawn, and it made me smile. Simon, assuming no one needed any help at the kitchen counter, soon joined me at the table. The letter. Every time I opened my mouth to tell them about it, I stopped. Simon solved the problem.

"So Clem, have you opened those letters yet?" He looked over at me, his eyebrows up.

"Yeah, I opened the first one this morning."

Mom stopped stirring the gorgonzola sauce for the gnocchi and looked over at me.

"Well?" she said, Aunt Julia and her head of bleached cotton candy sliding into view behind her.

"Uh, it's really confusing. But it's also kind of exciting. He wants me to open them in order and on some sort of timetable. Basically, he said that he wants, wanted, me to take a trip around the state. I guess there's something he wants me to know or understand or something . . ." I looked around at everyone looking at me and wished they would all just forget about the whole thing. "Um, so it looks like the next letter will tell me where to go first, then I open another letter when I get there. That sort of thing."

I pulled the first letter out of my back pocket and Mom unfolded it like it might explode in her face. Simon got up and crossed the kitchen in order to read the letter over her back, turning off the burner beneath the sauce on his way. Aunt Julia craned her neck enough to see the page as well and I sat silently while the three of them read the letter. As soon as Mom was finished, Simon took it from her hands, turned away from everyone, and read it again.

Aunt Julia piped up, "Well, I don't get it. Angie, does it make any sense to you?"

Mom was staring at some middle distance, not quite at the tiles on the floor.

"Ooh, you know what?" Julia asked the room of people not listening to her. "You could have a film crew follow you—like a reality show. That would be cool!"

"That might be interesting," Simon offered while leaning against the counter. He switched the gas flame back on underneath the sauce pan and started stirring.

"Forget about any film crew," I told them. "While I don't really get it, I think it might be kind of fun. I guess what's really throwing me is how weird it is to almost be talking to him, reading his words now. And I think about what it must have been like for him to write the letters. I mean, Mom? Did he ever tell you anything about this?"

Mom stared back at me. I could see the wheels turning in her head but had no idea what she might be trying to work out. She crossed her arms and spoke.

"I don't want you to do it."

I glanced at Simon, who looked as startled as I felt.

"What do you mean?"

"I mean, I don't want you to do this. Go ahead and read through the rest of the letters if you have to, but don't go on any trip and don't even think about telling me about any of it." Mom blew me a raspberry and walked out of the room.

Julia started after her, whispering on her way out of the kitchen, "It's okay, let me talk to her."

"What the fuck was that?" Simon asked.

He handed me the letter and I folded it back up, tucked it back into my pocket. I just shrugged at him and he went back to stirring the sauce. I sat there at the breakfast table for a few minutes, wondering what I had missed in all this. I'd read the letter a dozen times and nothing ever jumped out at me, made me think that Mom would get upset. This sort of rambling riddling was vintage Dad and I thought my mom would appreciate it. Maybe it was just too much for her to hear from him.

I got up and made my way to my parents' bedroom. The giant door to the room was ajar and I could see Mom sitting cross-legged on the ridiculously large four-poster bed, while Julia sat in the brocade wing chair by the window. Light filtered in through the eucalyptus trees outside and the whole room had its usual overstuffed, opulent feel. Marble and heavy fabrics and purposefully distressed wood and intricately woven rugs thick like animal pelts. They stopped talking when I walked in. I hadn't been in there since my dad died. Mom told me at the funeral how unsettling it was to sleep in the bed without Dad there. She said she was used to him being away but that she always knew he'd be back. Until now. I couldn't stop looking at his side of the bed. The last book he was reading still on the bedside table. His watch that he never wore but always kept out. The mound of pillows he referred to as "pillowtopia" stacked and ready for his angel head. When I did look away, I only saw some other reminder that this place was all Dad. His old sneakers at the entrance to the walk-in closet. The earplugs he left all over the place nesting in pairs on a bookshelf and a side table. He was nowhere now, but he was everywhere with us. Julia looked at Mom for a second and then left, saying she was going to get the dinner going again. I sat at the edge of the bed and faced my mother. She wasn't crying, but instead just looked shell-shocked.

"Mom, I—"

"Look, Sweetpea," she cut me off and then let out a sigh. "I just don't think that this game of Daddy's is going to help any of us and I would rather you not do it."

"But Mom, he obviously wanted me to do this."

"I know. But you have to ask yourself why."

"I have been. I don't know why, and I won't, unless I follow the letters. What are you afraid of?"

That last question seemed to pain her. Mom looked me in the eye for a long time and then leaned back against the headboard.

"It's different being the kid of someone like your dad than it is being the wife of someone like your dad." She looked away from me and out the window. "You don't understand how fragile faith and trust are when you are married to someone who is on the road all the time and who is constantly surrounded by people who don't give two shits about faith and trust."

"Are you ..." I started to ask, and then stopped myself.

"All I'm saying is that I have a bad feeling about this. Your father was, is, and always will be the love of my life. He never did anything at all to break that. And I don't want anything to break that now that he's gone, because then there will be no possibility of ever repairing it." She took a deep breath and looked back at me. "I don't know what Dad has out there that he wants you to find, but if it was something that couldn't be found while he was still around to deal with it, then there's no need to find it now."

I saw through all of Mom's verbal gymnastics that she was afraid of being betrayed. I didn't know if my mom was worried about illegitimate children or mistresses or something really vile, but I knew that she was protecting herself and her memory of my father. After all, that's all she had left of him.

"I don't know what to do, Mom." I looked down at the carpet and started to cry.

She reached down and took my hand.

"Do what you want, I guess. You're a grown woman. You make whatever decision you want. But know that if it were up to me, you'd forget about the whole thing. Take my feelings into account when you make up your mind."

And with that, she got up off the bed and headed downstairs. I stared at the dent she'd made in the bedding, wiped at my eyes with the backs of my hands, and then followed her back downstairs.

* * * * *

I drove home from dinner in a daze. I was sure I went down streets and turned left or right or waited at lights but wasn't really aware of any of it. All I could think of was Mom on the bed, staring out the window at her worst fears. Dad had been the sum total of her life and now she was worried it would all fall apart. I pulled into the driveway and sat in the car. I felt like hiding in the dark there forever. I'd spent the last three weeks wanting to hide away, wanting everything to be good again. I got through life like that, keeping a low profile and thinking about things. But now I felt like all the waiting just brought worse and worse shit my way. I started thinking of ways to make up my mind; some sort of chart, weigh the pros and cons. Too scientific. I thought about calling Simon or Dena, but tossed that idea as well. They wouldn't be able to see this situation any differently than I could.

I had three choices. I could go on the trip. I could not go on the trip. Or I could go on the trip, but just not tell anyone about it, particularly my mother. I started to think about that last option but then realized that if she ever found out about it, she'd only be hurt more. So now I was down to two options. Go, not go. If I went, there was the possibility that I'd find out something devastating. Or maybe I would find something wonderful. That was the unknown. If I didn't go, I would be going against what Dad wanted and would always wonder what was, but nothing would change. I thought about maybe just opening all of the letters, like skipping to the back of a book or having someone tell you the ending to a movie. But then that would be like going, right? *Right?*

Why couldn't someone just tell me what to do? Actually, they were. I had two people telling me. The two people I loved more than anything in the world telling me two different things. Fuck this. I sat there in the car in the driveway, banging my fists on the steering wheel and crying. I was crying for Dad and for how badly I wanted him back. I was crying for Mom and the bottomless hell she must have been feeling. Most of all, though, I was crying for me and my stupid life and my stupid uselessness.

I hadn't had an outburst like that since my scene at the reading of the will. I never unloaded like that ever, and it felt good. After a while I stopped crying, my hair plastered to my cheeks as my tears started to dry. I got out of the car and went inside, drained but relaxed. Sitting in the living room, just dead weight on the couch, I asked for a sign. Of course, I knew I could make this choice. I just needed something to push me there.

There was a rather idiotic game my friends and I used to play. I wish I could say I never really participated, that I just went along with whatever outcome was produced. But the truth is that I loved it. I loved the silliness and randomness even though I pretended to be above it all. If there was a decision to be made, we'd turn the radio on and hit the "seek" button a certain number of times (lucky number, birthday, age), and whatever came on the radio would be the answer to the question. "What should we have for lunch?" would be answered with twelve hits to the "seek" button, and when it landed on a station playing the *oompa oompa* of mariachi music, well, the answer was (of course) burritos. Sure, there were times when we landed on talk radio that couldn't be decoded right away. We would pick apart what we heard until the answer revealed itself. I know it sounds foolish but, looking back, I have to acknowledge that I never disagreed with the results.

It should be noted that it wasn't always trivial questions that were asked of the stereo. Sunny couldn't decide between going to UCLA or UC Santa Cruz. She had been debating the two for weeks when she suddenly turned the volume all the way down on the car radio as we drove back from a day in Venice. Sunny hit the button twenty-nine times, because her birthday is October 29, and when she turned the volume back up, "Los Angeles" by X was charging out of the speakers in the car. I was admittedly freaked out by the fate and chance of it all. Sunny screamed along with the lyrics as we headed back to her house where she filled out the registration form that came with her acceptance letter from UCLA. Sunny dropped out two years later, but still.

While I felt the game was stupid, absurd, and a bit rash, what in my life wasn't right then? I wanted a clear answer for this problem. I wanted someone, something in the great beyond, to give me that sign. I sat in the dark and, in a moment of clarity, thought about how any interpretation would be a sort of back-door view into my psyche anyway. I then also realized that I was getting really good with rationalization. I reached into my purse and pulled out my iPod, put the earbuds in, and figured that somewhere among the thousands of tracks was an answer. I could put it on shuffle and have something like Neil Young's "Old Man" start playing, or conversely, hear Mick Jagger's plaintive "Angie . . ." sing out at me. Music, it seemed, was my tarot, and I wanted all to be revealed.

I selected random play and held my breath. Quietly, familiar opening strains of guitar chords started building and were joined by the sound of my dad. The iPod had chosen my least favorite Condor song, the painfully titled "Warm Texas Rain."

Don't know what you'll do me for . . . but I know why I try . . .

It was an upbeat, jangley, banjo-riddled song about Dad going to Texas to win Mom back after a huge fight they had when they were young. It was about doing something difficult and not knowing what would come of it. It was freaking me out.

No choice now, I've got to go . . . wait for you in that warm Texas rain . . .

I made a mental note to get the car tuned up and make sure my AAA card was current. I hit pause and pulled out the earphones.

"Sorry, Mom," I whispered to the empty room.

CHAPTER FIVE

"All we know is still infinitely less than all that remains unknown."

—William Harvey

With my face washed and my teeth brushed, I climbed into bed. I sat up against the pillows and looked down at Letter Two in my hand.

"Okay, Dad. What have you got for me?" I slid my finger into the corner flap of the envelope and gently ripped it open.

Dear Clem,

You made it to the second letter! Hooo! Wowie Zowie!! Why don't you stop for a moment and take a nice deep breath? I'd do the same, but I don't think that, in the spirit world of the great beyond, breathing means anything at all. Okay. Holy shit, this is fun. Maybe it will get old soon, but I am digging the pretending-to-be-dead game.

Fact: There is a lot of feminine energy in my music. This is because I love women and what they bring to the cosmic table. I love their smell, their taste, their sound, their magic! There's a mystery to you ladies that can't be understood, but I just try to feel it and let it come to me, flow through me. The main mysterious lady of my life is, as you know, your mother. Wondering about her magic and her love possessed me and sparked creativity in me. You know the story about "Loving Rose"? That the song is all about her. Everyone knows that. But here's something for the trivia books: I'm about to tell you the story behind the story.

You know I met your mother in San Francisco. You know we moved to Los Angeles together in, what was it, 1968, '69? We didn't have anything at all in those days. We drove down to LA in a '58 Chevy with two paper sacks full of our clothes in the back. That was it. We took our time driving down, partly to enjoy the trip and partly because we kept getting lost. It was summertime, and the heat was incredible. Most of the time the car smelled like musky sweat and the ripe fruit your mother kept buying from roadside stands. It was wonderful.

We stopped in a little town called Wasco, smack-bang in the middle of their annual Rose Festival. There were roses everywhere and people bustling and laughter. The air was perfumed with flowers and humanity. We wandered around the festival that afternoon, and that night we slept in the car on the edge of a field of rosebushes. We stretched out across the backseat with the windows open and listened to some guys play Mexican folk songs on guitars somewhere in the warm night. Life was a dream that night, and every day and night after that. I wrote "Loving Rose" that night in my head. Kept it all up there, and when we hit LA, we went right to Jerry's house and I wrote it all down on a scrap of that lined school paper. Jerry and I formed Condor right then and there.

I want you to go to Wasco. It's just off the 99 a ways. It doesn't matter if the festival is on or not. I want you to go to the town and feel that energy that I absorbed. It's the seed of us, the family and the music, and it's a good place to start. Sit at the edge of a field of roses and feel all the vibrations around you. Live it, Clem, and when you have, you'll know that life is a dream. When you are there, and you think you are ready, then you can open the next letter. But take your time and soak it all up. It's there for the taking.

xo,

Dad

My heart sunk with his mention of "feminine energy," but I recovered at the mention of Mom. But what did he mean by "*main* mysterious lady"? What I took as Mom's paranoia was now leaking into me as slight, but genuine, concern. What if she was onto something? I read the letter two more times and determined that I would take the text at face value. Dad wanted me to go to Wasco, I was going to Wasco. Wherever the hell it was.

I slept that night without dreaming until the sun shining on my face became too warm to ignore and I opened my eyes again. Everything was still there. The letter was still in a tent fold on the bedside table. Dad was still gone. I spent forty-five minutes of my morning spacing out and then got down to the business of getting ready for this trip into the unknown.

I was digging through the trunk for the road atlas I knew was in there somewhere when Sunny called. She wanted to tell me about the weird dream she'd had the night before. Sunny did this a lot, repeating the nonsense of her dreams to anyone who would listen. I never had the heart to tell her that I just didn't care. Quite honestly, dreams are so personal and distorted that they really can't be of interest to anyone but the dreamer. But whenever Sunny had a weird one, she made sure to tell me all about it. The details of this one seemed to go on forever, drifting from one scenario to the next. At last, she was done.

"Weird, huh? What do you think falling through that wall of green pillows means?"

"I don't know, Sun."

The atlas was wedged under some stiff beach towels. I grabbed it and took the towels inside the house for a well-deserved wash.

"Me neither. What did you dream last night?"

"I opened the second letter last night."

I told Sunny about the dinner at Mom's and her freak-out about the letter.

"That doesn't sound like your mom. Besides, you read me the letter and it didn't seem all that crazy. I mean, it was intense, but I didn't get anything *ominous* out of it."

"Yeah, but after last night, ominous is all I can think about. I'm still doing the trip, though."

"Do you want me to go with you? I can have someone watch the store. It's really no problem."

"Thanks, but I think I need to do this myself. Don't worry, I'll email and call you the whole time."

"I'd be mad if you didn't. I'm serious. If you need me or if you need anything at all, you let me know."

How could I ask for something if I didn't even know what I needed? The one person who could answer my questions was gone.

"Hey, Clem, why don't you come over? A bunch of us are sitting around the pool. We were going to go to The Roosevelt and swim there, but you know it'll be all crawling with fucking reality show people and not anyone good. Anyway, we're here at my apartment if you want to come by."

"Thanks, but I think I'll pass."

I hung up with Sunny and sat on the floor of my kitchen.

* * * * *

I decided to give myself a week before starting out for Wasco. Dramatic, sure, but I wanted to see if any real doubt would creep into my head about the whole thing. I wanted to give my mother the opportunity to change her mind and give the trip her blessing. I wanted one more chance at this being a joke, or a dream, or something other than my new reality.

I used that week to prepare or, more accurately, obsessively orchestrate to the nth degree. Maps, accident claim forms, health insurance cards, gas station credit cards, a first aid kit, more maps, names and addresses of anyone I knew anywhere in the state . . . it all sat in neat piles on the kitchen table, ready to be stored in the car when I did actually leave. Of course, all I knew about the trip was the first leg, a stretch of highway one hundred and forty miles long. After that, it was all sealed envelopes.

Dena called every day, excited about the trip and full of new theories about Dad and the letters. Her ideas were all hidden treasure or historical drama, no scandal at all. She was sure Mom's objections were based on "her issues with memory ownership." She said she could *feel* that Dad would send me up to the Bay Area at some point, and we made plans to see each other while I was there. If I went there. Dena talked a lot about positivity and the soul. I knew Dena was better suited to this sort of thing than I was. Maybe that was the point.

Simon called too, suggesting every time that I open all the letters right then. The closer I got to leaving, the more his calls consisted of him barking at me in a stern voice to open the letters. He wanted me to read them all to him right there on the phone. I couldn't help but laugh at his calls, which seemed to irritate him a little. But I thought he also enjoyed talking to me on a daily basis, something out of the ordinary for us. The truth was that I did still sometimes think about opening all of the letters and trying to get a grasp of what was ahead of me. This letter-by-letter approach was all Dad and in no way me. This wasn't about me, though, so the letters stayed sealed.

* * * * *

Mom and Simon came over the night before I left. They walked in carrying Thai takeout, all smiles and cheer. They sat in the kitchen, ate dinner, and tried really hard to be breezy and casual, like it was before we lost Dad.

"Julia said it was eighty-five degrees out when her plane landed in Dallas Sunday morning. Eighty-five at ten in the morning. Oh, I don't miss Texas at all," Mom said, laughing.

"How are her lips?" Simon asked while spooning more green curry onto his plate.

"Her what?"

I was confused, and wondered with a cringe if Julia's glossy collagen lips hadn't survived high-altitude flight, pressurized cabins or not.

"Oh, Jul had her lips done on Monday after she got back, and she said that they were a little swollen. She's fine now."

Simon looked over at me and pulled his lower lip as far out as he could while wiggling his eyebrows. Mom slapped him on the arm.

"Cut it out. It's not like the girls you run around with haven't seen a scalpel or two in their day."

"Touché, Mom."

Simon took a small cube of fried sweet potato off his plate and put it on Mom's, like some sort of peace offering. It had been a while since I had seen him silly like this and I liked it. I missed it.

We piled the plates into the dishwasher and stacked the waxed-paper takeout boxes on the counter. Mom made a couple of swipes over the table with a dish rag, more for motherly show than any actual cleaning. I thought this was sweet and couldn't help but reach from behind her and put my arms around her. Simon came up and made motions like he was about to pick her up by the feet. Mom squealed and we laughed. There wasn't a way for me to love my family any more than I did at that moment.

Mom and Simon stuck around for another half hour or so, Simon attempting to keep the conversation light by telling stories he'd heard from clients in exotic locations.

"Yeah, and then Carrie was telling me about Amazonian wood-eating fish. She said they just cruise around the bottom of the river, eating wood."

"There's a crude joke in there somewhere," Mom pointed out. We all knew that Dad would have been the one to make it.

"Oh, *har har*. What I don't understand is how a creature can get nutrients from a water-soaked log. I mean, if it's eating the wood to get the algae and microorganisms and shit, wouldn't it be easier just to filter it out of the water like other fish?"

"I heard ballerinas eat tissues to feel full but not gain weight, and they are still able to run and jump and dance around on their bashed-up toes. Maybe there is nutritional value in wood pulp." I didn't believe this but I was enjoying all this talk about nothing and wanted to keep it going.

"I think that's an urban legend, Clem."

"I think you should wait until I die to go on the trip." Mom stared at me.

We all stopped. The clock on the wall ticked into the empty air she had created. I looked from Mom to Simon, who was looking from Mom to me.

"Mom," I told her, "I'm going. It's nothing against you. I thought you were going to be okay with this."

"I mean it. Just wait until I'm dead. I know you feel you have a duty and I understand that. But—"

Simon put his arm around her.

"Mom, stop."

She looked at Simon and then at me. She was defeated, and I felt shitty for it. Still, my mind was made up. There was a long silence then Simon announced they should get going. As they got up to leave, I could see that my mom was trying not to cry. Instead she started digging in her purse. I walked out to Simon's car with them and as I hugged Mom goodbye, she whispered in my ear.

"You sure you won't wait until I'm dead too?"

"Sorry, Mom."

I hugged her tight.

"Well, then. Go on your trip. Leave me here with Simon and his stupid fucking fish stories."

I laughed at her valiant effort to erase the tension. She opened the passenger door to Simon's Porsche but stopped and looked back at me.

"I may be pissed off, but I'm still your mom, so call me if you need anything." She brushed her hand on my cheek. "I love you."

I repeated my love back and watched as they drove away, until the back of Simon's car whipped around a corner and they were gone.

I cleaned up all the takeout containers, making sure to put them in the trash cans on the side of the house. I could only imagine the smells that would come from Thai food left out for . . . And then, suddenly, it hit me that I had no idea how long I would be gone. It's not as if I had anywhere to be or anything else to do, but it would have been nice to know how much stuff to bring with me. I went into the living room, sat at the piano, and gently played out Dave Brubeck's "Take Five." I'd played it so often that I didn't even think about the notes, they just came off my hands. I thought about the trip and figured I couldn't be gone for more than a week and a half. There were only eight letters, and I couldn't see how I'd need to spend more than an entire day in each place. It wasn't like I was heading into the Yukon. If I needed anything, I could just buy it. I stopped mid-bar and looked up. *Please, Dad, make everything turn out okay.* I got up and began packing.

* * * * *

I started out toward Wasco the next day. It was gray in the early morning but by the time I got on the road, the sun was burning off the cloud cover and the temperature was warming up. I left a note on the kitchen counter thanking Sunny for looking after the mail and the plants, and gave the jasmine bush one last soaking before putting my bag in the trunk and locking everything up. I was nervous and had hoped the feeling would fade when I got in the car, but no such luck. It was the kind of day in LA that made me want to shine along with it—all sun and possibility. I navigated the freeways and the remnants of that morning's rush hour, taking in all the houses and strip malls and office buildings like it was the first time I'd seen them. Before I knew it, the Angeles National Forest was to my right, Los Padres to my left, and Pyramid Lake up ahead. I was on my way out of the LA basin at last.

Before driving down the Grapevine, I pulled into Gorman and its cluster of gas stations and fast food restaurants. I wanted some gum and also needed to just stop the car and take some deep breaths. I'd been driving for about an hour and was still a little edgy—this was surely going to be a long fucking trip if I couldn't pull myself together. As I parked in the lot of a massive gas station, I saw something hanging from the rear hitch of a truck parked a few spaces away. It gleamed silver but I couldn't tell exactly what it was. I got out of the car and walked toward the station's mini-mart but slowed to peer at this hanging thing on my way. Closer inspection proved the item to be something resembling testicles. Massive, veiny balls the size of grapefruits. Hanging from the truck. It was like looking at an un-neutered bulldog from behind, family jewels swaying to and fro.

"Hey there!"

A cheery man's voice sang out to me from the front of the truck. I looked up and saw a guy in a captain's hat smoking a cigarette and cleaning his windshield.

"Hi," I answered and kept walking toward the store. I could see my reflection in his aviator glasses.

"Admiring my nuts, were ya?"

The man chuckled, flicked his cigarette to the ground, and mashed it out with his sneaker. "They're called Bumper Nuts. Pretty funny, eh? I got 'em in a truck stop in Barstow."

"Yeah."

I didn't know what else to say to the guy. I'd stopped walking and now it looked like I was about to get into a conversation about vehicle scrotum.

"My name's Pappy."

The man kept his distance and just raised a hand in a wave.

"I'm Clem, nice to meet you," I waved back and started walking toward the store again.

"They sell them in pink too. They look realistic! You should get some!"

"I'll think about it," I called out to him as I walked away.

I made it into the shop and bought a pack of spearmint gum and some lemonade. I could still see Pappy and his huge silver balls out in the lot. I stuck my head out the glass double doors and called out to him.

Now, there are people in the world who are always trying to initiate conversation. I am not one of those people. I am the person those people are hoping to stumble across. I will never just keep walking. I can't. Pappy seemed like he wanted to talk and I was in no hurry.

"Hey, Pappy! You want anything from the store?"

This was the kind of shit I always did. The kind of thing that most of my friends and half of my family found really irritating.

"Uh, yeah. Could you get me a tall boy of Bud and a pepperoni stick?"

"Coming right up!" I yelled back.

Moments later, we were sitting on the blue metal picnic bench just outside the store.

"Thanks, Clem. What do I owe ya?" Pappy was reaching into his back pocket for his wallet.

"It's on me. Next time you meet someone who's in need of a drink and some processed meat, just pass it on."

"Very *New Age* of you." He took a swig of the beer and set it on the tabletop. "So where you headed?"

"Wasco. You?"

"Oh, I'm coming down from Winters to see my brother in Brawley."

"Where's that?"

"Brawley? Just south of the Salton Sea. Kind of near the Chocolate Mountains, that aerial bombing range. I figure I'll take the 5 into LA, then take the 10 out to Indio, then pick up the 86 through to Brawley."

"That's a long way. It's going to be pretty hot there too."

"Oh, you bet it is! My brother owns a hardware store there. He's got an air conditioner that won't quit!" Pappy took a long pull from the can. "I'm heading down there to help him with some remodeling he wants to do in the store. Got to keep up the competitive edge with all the big superstores out there, you know?"

"I hear you. So is that what you do?"

"No, I'm retired. Put in thirty years as a Yolo County Sheriff's Deputy. Spent the last twelve of those years sitting on my duff, watching people set off the courthouse metal detectors with pocket knives and steel-toe boots. But it was good work, good benefits. How about you?"

I hated this question. Sometimes I lied, told people I was a chiropractor or a taxidermist or used the ubiquitous rich kid catch-all: handbag designer. I couldn't think of anything worthwhile and Pappy seemed like a good guy, someone I wouldn't really want to lie to.

"I don't really do anything right now. Unemployed, I guess you'd say."

Pappy looked over to my car.

"Looks like unemployment is treating you pretty well."

I let this hang, not sure if I could tell him anything that would make him see me as anything other than spoiled and useless.

"I had a generous dad," was all I could muster.

That was the first time I'd put my father in the past tense without thinking about it first. At that moment, there in the gas station parking lot, I realized he really was gone.

"Lucky girl."

"Yeah, I am."

Pappy finished his beer and I put the top back on my bottle of lemonade, now half-empty and sweating condensation down its sides. We wished each other well and headed toward our cars.

"You have a safe drive to Wasco, Clem."

"I will. You drive safe too."

I watched Pappy's truck and its silver nuts pull out of the parking lot and get onto the freeway. Off we went in different directions. I had no idea what I was doing, where I was going. Pappy knew exactly where he was off to and was going just the same. I thought about Dad and felt a little guilty for putting him aside for a moment while I listened to Pappy and his story. But that's what Dad wanted me to do, go out there and see and hear and feel. I could see and hear and feel and vibrate and transcend and whatever the hell else he wanted, but at the end of the day, he would still be gone and I'd still be . . . whatever it is I am. I pulled onto the freeway and headed north.

CHAPTER SIX

WASCO

"Caught somewhere between the road and the Rose of San Joaquin"

—Tom Russell

It was just after noon when I reached Wasco. Dad was right about the roses—they were everywhere. Planted in the median of the main street, ringing houses, clumped in front of businesses, painted on the water tower. I could understand why my mom wanted to stop there. Her rose garden is massive, filled with roses of every variety and name. Hybrid teas and heirloom English and Floribunda, Glamis Castle and Change of Heart and Black Magic. She thinks roses are perfect. She loves the scent and the waxiness of the leaves and all the meanings behind colors and names. But more than anything, she loves that the flowers aren't symmetrical, that the petals at the heart are often misshapen, imperfect. That, to her, is perfection.

For as long as I can remember, longer than that, I suppose, Dad had roses delivered to my mother. The florist van would appear like clockwork on the drive every week bearing another dozen. Special occasions warranted enormous bouquets, bunches that sometimes barely fit through the front door. But always roses. I didn't know if the florist would still bring the roses and if Mom would still want them and if the roses would make her feel like Dad was still around or only make her miss him more.

I was getting hungry and still hadn't seen any picturesque rose fields, so I stopped at a taqueria for something to eat. The smell of the place made me ravenous and I could hardly wait for a foil wrapped *torta* to come my way. The place was full of construction workers on their lunch breaks and giggling high school students in sweatshirts with "Home of the Tigers!" inked across the back. I squeezed past everyone and slipped into the restroom while the busy cooks behind the counter assembled burritos and tacos and hilarious one-liners in Spanish.

As I was washing my hands, two teenage girls brushed past; one ducking into a stall and the other pausing next to me at the sink. I looked up and watched in the mirror as she gently applied another coat of soft pink to her lips, brushed her bangs to the side. She caught my eye in the mirror and I smiled at her but the girl just stared back. The look she gave me made me feel plucked out of everything in that instant. I felt like I was intruding, didn't belong. This was just a pissy kid but I felt singled out and alone. I headed back out to the restaurant right as my number was called.

I got my *torta*, made my way down the street, and sat on a bench in the shade. I could hear the laughs and screams from a school playground somewhere nearby. Some sullen-looking teenagers sat in a truck parked not far away, smoking cigarettes and listening to the heavy crunches and bleats of some nü metal band. Middle of the day in the middle of the week. Everyone must have been at work. I tried to imagine myself in an office or behind a register or at a factory. A woman walked toward me, pushing a baby in a bright blue stroller. She glanced at me as she passed, pinching out a weak smile. I smiled back, from her to the baby and then her again, wondering what I must look like. For that instant, I saw myself outside of myself. I saw me and my car and my letters and my grief and my confusion. I saw how ridiculous I must seem to everyone else in the world. Sitting on that bench, I figured all of the drama, the "Jasper family opera" as Sunny called it, meant nothing in the grand scheme of things. But it was still pulling me apart. From the outside, everything looks easy. But it never is, no matter who you are.

I was headed back to the car but decided instead to wander around the town a little first, walk off the delicious grease of my lunch. There wasn't much there, but I felt oddly drawn to the calm of such a small town and wanted to feel like I could just blend right in. I wondered what it would be like to live somewhere like this, kind of aside from the rest of things. What would it be like to have the Circle K as your hangout instead of the club of the moment or the Chateau Marmont? Would I still be the same person if I'd grown up here? In the whole nature/nurture argument, one hundred and forty miles is a world away.

I stopped at a fruit stand on the sidewalk and selected a small basket of strawberries for the ride to wherever came next. I thought about a guy Dad knew who was a really successful singer in the early eighties. The guy raised his family on a farm in rural England, far away from any nightlife or drooling fans. One of his sons is a quiet guy who is studying to be a veterinarian and whose idea of a wild night out is a pub quiz and fish and chips before midnight. The other son is a borderline junky who just moved from London to New York because he knew his name would get him further there. I am pretty sure we all become who we're supposed to be in the end.

I paid for the berries, then got back in the car and started looking for a field of roses to sit by and absorb whatever it was I was supposed to absorb. I clumsily navigated the even grid of Wasco's streets, and a few minutes later I was just outside the center of town and scanning for a place to park and sit. I'd imagined soft fields and wide, cushiony tufts of velvety earth. I'd imagined wrong. The fields were hard lines that ran right up to the road. On my right seemed an endless stretch of jagged green leaves and pouting buds.

Roses, all in an oddly orderless jumble of varieties and color. It was a strangely overwhelming tableau of Technicolor agribusiness, the soft and the hard at odds but as one. I pulled onto the shoulder, got out, and sat cross-legged in the dirt, Letter Two resting in my lap. Nettles and poppies fanned the edge of the tilled ground, the only natural and unplanned thing on site. The exact sneaking wild that Dad would have loved.

I took a deep breath, expecting rose essence to fill my nose and lungs, to deliver Dad's intent. Instead, all I could smell was oil and dust and the green smell of manure drifting over the fields. I figured there was a dairy nearby, since it didn't look like the roses had been freshly fertilized. It was unpleasant sitting in the gravelly dirt, tiny stones poking into my ass, surrounded by dusty grit from the road, buzzing wasps, and the smell of shit. I started to get up when a large white truck pulled off the highway and onto the shoulder in front of my car. It startled me, and I fell back into sitting again.

A young guy in a brown uniform got out and headed toward me.

"You okay?"

"Uh, yeah, I'm fine." I got up and brushed dirt off the seat of my pants.

"I saw you sitting here and thought maybe there was some problem."

"No. No problem. I was just, uh, thinking." As I said this, he looked down at my hand and Dad's letter clutched in it.

I read the patch on his sleeve: California Department of Corrections. He caught me looking and smiled.

"I work at the state prison." He pointed toward a low, sprawling structure in the distance. "Pensive-looking women on the side of the road are a dime a dozen for us. So what's he in for?"

He looked at me with a tenderness I wouldn't normally associate with a prison warden. I started to laugh.

"No, no, this isn't from anyone in jail. I don't know anyone in prison. Um, this is a letter from my dad. He died a few weeks ago." I looked back down at the letter.

"Oh, sorry. Sorry about your dad. But it's still probably not too safe to sit on the side of the highway."

"I know. It's just that he sort of wanted me to—" I cut myself short. It didn't matter to this guy what Dad wanted. Nothing mattered.

"Are you sure you're okay?" He was looking into the car now, scanning the interior then staring at the strawberries.

"Yeah. I'm cool." I reached through the open window of the passenger seat and pulled out the basket of berries. "Want one?"

The warden looked at me and smiled.

"Actually, yeah. Thanks." He reached over and plucked two from my hand. "My grandfather used to pick these." He held one up. "All day, that's what he did."

"That's tough work."

"It was." He looked out over the rose field.

"I think my grandfather grew asparagus, canned it or something."

"Really? Where?"

"I don't know. My dad never really talked about it. It was somewhere north of here, but I don't know where."

"It's funny, my dad never eats strawberries because he says they remind him of his father, aching and broken at the end of the day and smelling like sweat and dirt. Real flair for the dramatic, my pop."

He bit into the berry and then tossed the hull toward the field. "Mine, too."

"Sounds like it, with a letter on the side of a two-lane highway and all."

We both chuckled and each ate another strawberry in silence.

"The thing about my dad is that his father picked all those berries so he wouldn't have to. My dad's never worked outside an office. He gets angry over work he's never done."

"Well, maybe he's still holding on to your grandfather's anger," I suggested, looking at the warden, but thinking about the empty spaces in my own family history.

"Nah, Grandpa wasn't angry. My dad's just hurt, but I'm proud. I'm proud of the work my grandpa did. He worked hard. It's like Cesar Chavez said: 'Children of farm workers should be as proud of their parents' professions as other children are of theirs.' Grandpa believed in *La Causa*, for sure," he chuckled. "Sorry to suddenly ramble on like that. I've just been thinking about it a lot lately, I guess."

"Hey, I understand."

"And I want my grandkids, when I have them someday, to be proud of the work I do too."

"They will be."

"Well, corrections officers aren't exactly the most popular people, you know." He laughed at his own admission.

We finished off the berries and looked out over the field.

"Thanks for stopping to check on me. That was really nice of you."

"No problem. It's what I do. So where are you headed?"

I held up the letter. "We shall see."

"Well, good luck and have a safe trip."

I thanked him, said goodbye, and watched him as he got back in his truck and sped off toward the prison.

I got back in the car, reached into my purse, and pulled out Letter Three. With Wasco accomplished in half a day, I started to think that maybe this wouldn't be as long and arduous as I'd originally expected. I settled back into the seat, the sun-warmed leather sending sleepiness through my back.

Precious Clem,

So how did Wasco treat you? Were the roses in bloom? Did you inhale all the beauty? It's a nice place, huh?

Okay. So you've done the Loving Rose portion of the trip. No, I'm not making you drive the equivalent of a Greatest Hits album. Although that's not a bad idea for the fan club. The Condorks should organize something like that. Don't they have Beatles tours in London? I'll tell your mother to look into that.

Anyway, life in the early days was rough. Your mom and I moved to LA because San Francisco was starting to get too heavy for us and because Jerry had moved down six months earlier and said it was a paradise. He liked LA because you got all the drugs and the music and the women and the good times without all of the serious shit like politics and social responsibility and whatnot that was all over SF. I have to say that I agreed with him a little bit. But more on that later.

So I moved to LA, and we started the band and played just about every craphole in town. We loaded all the equipment into a van and started playing every craphole in the state. We heard from a buddy of mine that the summertime was good for playing county fairs and stuff like that. You would get paid pretty well (pretty well for those days) and they would give you free booze and food. Not bad. So we would try and hit as many of those as we could.

California was changing back then, but it was also a lot like it is now. There are some fucking rural *places out there in our Golden State. Believe me. And some of those places didn't really care for long-haired musical spirits like myself.*

I'd like to think I've only been in a few real fights in my life. One time was in New Orleans in 1987, when I yelled at a guy for kicking his dog and he started kicking me instead. But let's focus on this next one.

I was in Clovis. We were booked to play the "Big Hat Festival" there. I am not shitting you, darling daughter, when I tell you that the festival was all about wearing big fucking hats. It was wild! We'd been playing all over the place, all the way up to Seattle and back, and Clovis was our last stop before we got back to LA. I was exhausted, bringing music to the cracks and nooks and hidey-holes of the world. But something about the silliness of this Clovis gig just got to me, you know? I was in love with it. The silliness romanced me! We played the songs *that made up that first album of ours (*Chuggin' On*) and some covers of old blues tunes. The folks loved us. It was like there was all this joy around, and they fed it to us, and we fed it to them, until the air and the dirt and the big pots of chili were all just joy and happiness.*

After the show, me and the boys wanted to keep spreadin' the joy, if you know what I mean, so we went to this little bar off the highway. I think the place was called Shitkickers. No, it wasn't. But it should have been. We were in the bar for about ten minutes when three big farm boys started talking to me. Seems Rick and I had been talking to some girls who were their sisters or girlfriends (probably both! Ha ha ha). They didn't like that, and they didn't like how my pants were tight and that it was apparent I wasn't wearing any underwear. They didn't like my long hair or my rings. They were threatened. I tried to reason with them, to share the joy. They didn't want the joy.

A bit of a tussle broke out and before I knew it, I was being tossed toward the door. That would have been fine by me, as I just wanted to get the hell out of there. But instead I found myself going at it with the door frame . . . and the frame won. My face hit the wood, and the next thing I knew, I was in the back of the van missing a tooth. Motherfuckers, I was mad! Turns out my tooth got embedded in the door. I was so empty of all the good feelings I had earlier. I started to wonder if maybe everything I was doing was a mistake. I thought maybe I'd be better off being one of the world's milk-fed farm boys than one of the world's slithering voices of the spirits. Then I realized that the only thing I could be was me. And that the only way I could be was how I was. I decided right then and there to put that violence behind me and to take my music so far and to so many people that we would become the majority. I also wanted to be so rich that the dentist bill from the broken tooth would be nothing but chump change. Ha ha!

I never went back to Clovis. Rick went back there, back to the bar where all the shit went down. The old shack had been torn down, so he didn't get my tooth back for me. But he spit on the ground in front of the place. He also pissed on the wall and got that citation, the one that he never paid and had the warrant for. So while I want you to go to Clovis, I don't want you pissing on any walls.

Go to Clovis (I think it may have been swallowed up by Godforsaken Fresno by now) and see where I was able to be a spiritual alchemist. 27 Kern Street. I took golden emotion that had turned to shit and turned it back into gold again. Go to Clovis and realize that there's always a way to spin things back in your favor. There's always a way to bring the joy back from the dead.

Don't worry, Clem. This trip is just building up. There's a lot more to come.

xoox,

Dad

That's what I was afraid of.

CHAPTER SEVEN

CLOVIS

"Dread of night. Dread of not-night."

—Fran Kafka

I drove back toward the 99 on the straightaway of Highway 46 that brought me to Wasco just a couple of hours before. Slow-moving tractors tried to gain pace on the shoulder with the passing traffic, cutting onto the road when a break opened up. Moving, everything is always moving, and it seemed like I was too. For the first time, I felt like I was moving.

I followed the exit and string of roads as indicated on the driving itinerary I'd looked up on my Blackberry. I perched the road atlas, which I discovered was at least twenty-five years old, on the passenger seat. Its tiny curving lines, red dashes, and black dot cities corroborated the Internet directions. Still, for a few miles off the freeway, I was sure I'd gone the wrong way. I seemed to be driving into nothingness, just tract homes and fields. I crossed the railroad tracks, the Golden State Boulevard, streets and overpasses, and miles of dirt. Then there was Clovis.

It was a cool little town, like something dropped there from the Midwest. I tried to picture it when Dad was here and figured it was pretty much the same, just newer cars. I drove around for a bit and then found my destination. Sort of.

It should have been there, 27 Kern Street. But the exact address seemed to have been absorbed by what could best be described as a strip mall that grew up into a bunch of offices. Not a dirty drinking hole in sight. Just on the edge of the Clovis Old Town, the new building had the same broad elevated sidewalks in front of it but without any of the old-style charm. I parked the car, got out, and leaned back against the hood. So this was where Dad got his ass kicked. I tried to imagine the scene but with the stenciled-glass front windows and aluminum trim doors, I just couldn't see it.

"Can I help you?"

I looked over and saw a middle-aged woman coming out of the real estate office. I guess I had been standing there for a while and probably looked lost.

"No, I'm alright, thanks. I was just thinking. Actually, maybe you *can* help me. Did there used to be a bar here? A while back?"

She smiled and came down the two steps off the sidewalk and stood beside me. She was wearing an aggressively pink suit with matching heels. As she got closer, her perfume hovered in the air around us. I thought it was something I liked the smell of, but would never wear myself. There was a tiny gold pin on her lapel that said "Happiness is an inside job!" I didn't know what that was all about, but I thought it was something Dad would have been into.

"Oh, yeah. There was a bar here. I used to go there from when I was a teenager. Well, until it closed. That was almost . . ." She paused to think. "Twenty, twenty-five years ago, maybe? Long time ago. I like your sunglasses, by the way."

This lady was sort of intense, but also kind of entertaining.

"Oh, thanks. Huh. Do you remember what it was called, the bar?"

"Sure! For years it was called the Ice House. Then, toward the end of the seventies, they changed the name to the Condor Bar. It was a wild place back then." She shook her head side to side a little to indicate just how wild, I guess.

"Condor Bar?" I couldn't believe it.

"Yeah, the Condor. Like the band, huh? I mean, it wasn't named after the band, I don't think. You heard about the singer dying, right? Oh my god, isn't that horrible? I mean, he was still young! So sad."

Holy shit. It didn't occur to me that people would still be talking about Dad. I swallowed hard and stared at the ground.

"Yeah, it's sad."

"You're probably too young to remember them. But you know, I had a little groupie brush with fame with those guys."

My stomach dropped. This was too fucking much, and I couldn't say anything at all, just raised my eyebrows and braced myself against the car.

"Sure! It was back in '79 or so. Some girlfriends and I drove down to LA to see them play. They were *really* popular then. We got all dolled up and were just wild, you know?" She did the little head shake again, her bangs whipping back and forth across her forehead. "We were all waiting outside the back entrance to the arena, hanging out with a couple other girls who wanted to meet the band. Some roadies let us backstage, and my friend Kristi, uh, *serviced* the drummer in the bathroom! Can you believe that? He was the only guy from the band back there and my God, he knew how to party. Wow, I haven't thought about that in ages." She sighed and looked off into the distance.

The moment I heard "drummer," relief rushed through me, and I started coughing to cover the huge exhale I'd been holding in.

"You okay?" The woman looked at me with concern.

"Yeah, I think it's just allergies or something. That's a pretty crazy story, with the drummer and all."

"Oh, yeah. We did lots of crazy stuff back then. But that was a long, long time ago and I left all that behind. I had a kid, a little boy, and I just couldn't raise him and be that person. So nineteen years ago, when Ronnie—that's my son—was four years old, I gave up all the smoking and drinking and partying for good. Haven't had any since."

"Good for you. That's really great."

"Yeah. Almost twenty years sober. I got myself together, finished up my associate's degree, and then got my real estate license. Not bad, huh?"

"Not bad at all."

"That's the American Dream, isn't it? But I think it's even more the California dream. The American Dream is all about becoming whatever you want. But in California, you can *remake* yourself into whatever you want, you know? I don't think in most places I could have gone from the person I was to the person I am now. I'm lucky."

This lady in the loud suit was nice, but holy shit, was she over-sharing.

"That's the truth. Life is full of second chances here."

"And third and fourth and fifth . . ." She laughed. "So, where are you from, and what brings you looking for some old bar?"

"Oh, I live in LA. The bar was just some place my dad told me about, and I wanted to see for myself."

"Well, if you ever decide you want to move up here, I'm the real estate agent for you."

She reached into the inside pocket of her jacket and pulled out a card. I wanted to think this whole routine of hers was a way to hone in on the lady leaning on a Mercedes outside her office, but it seemed more a sincere gesture and not like some hard sell. Maybe that was her secret. I decided to believe that her openness was for real and took the card from her hand. *Tina O'Brian, for all your real estate needs* in glossy print, next to a picture of Tina holding a comically serious expression on her face, framed by her long blonde hair and an incredible amount of makeup.

"Thanks. You know, it was really nice talking to you. And I promise that if I ever decide to move here, you'll be the first person I call."

"You do that. Oh." She reached out her hand to shake mine. "I didn't get your name."

I froze. Would she recognize my name?

"It's Clem. Clem Benedetto."

I used Mom's maiden name. Tina the real estate lady could be honest, but I wanted to be comfortable.

"Nice to meet you, Clem."

I thanked her again and left. It was getting later in the day and I figured it would be best to get some hotel room now instead of driving to wherever. I headed back toward the freeway and found a Comfort Tree Inn just off the 99.

Roadside motels always seem sort of cool and romantically seedy in the abstract. In the concrete, the Comfort Tree Inn was neither. It was a sterile place, all buzzing fluorescent lights and tight-pile maroon carpeting. There seemed to be a lot of agribusiness guys staying there—suits in cowboy hats. I got a room and stretched out on the bed for a while, staring at the ceiling. The ceiling anywhere is such a blank canvas, and I thought I should be able to see something in it. That's why I always stared. But all I saw were the pebble stipples of spray plaster, continuous and rough.

I went downstairs through the small lobby and headed outside to the restaurant that sat across the wide parking lot. It was some chain place, prefabricated and held at a standard that was passable for most of America. I didn't feel like sitting alone there. Eating by myself in a place didn't bother me, it's just that I was already feeling kind of lonely and I thought the whole "table for one" thing would just make me wallow in it. I ordered a club sandwich to go and went back up to my room.

I sat on the bed and in between bites of the sandwich and limp fries read and answered the emails that were stacking up on my Blackberry. Mom telling me she heard there was a big rig accident on the 10 and to be careful driving. Dena talking about letting go in order to communicate with Dad's spirit. Sunny listing off who was at some club the night before and complaining about how she didn't know if some guy was her boyfriend yet or not. Simon asking to know what's going on.

I wish I knew, I wrote back to Simon. I meant it. I shared my itinerary so far with everyone. I told Mom that it was shaping up to be a harmless trip and not to worry. I told Dena and Sunny about the people I met. I suggested Sunny ask the guy she was sleeping with about the boyfriend issue. I broadcasted all the information I had and then opened Letter Four.

Dear Clem,

Motivation. That's a word that's been co-opted and absorbed by the corporate machine and hack actors everywhere. But it's an important thing, motivation. A person has to understand the motivation of others and in their own soul. It's the why*, baby, that gets us every time.*

We are all connected to a place, whether we like it or not. That connection remains even if we try to change who we are. The land and the air fill us with energies, some that never escape us. I started out life connected to a place and an energy that were, well shit, they were difficult. It wasn't for me. I'm not sure it was for anyone. But it's where I started out, and that can't be erased.

I was born in Walnut Grove. I don't think you've ever been there. Truth is, I don't think you know much about my side of the family at all. That's how I wanted it. I like to think that I was just dropped from the ether one day, that I don't have any ties to anything other than the family I've created. But there ain't no stork and we all come from somewhere.

All that family up there is long dead. Even longer dead by the time you'll be reading these letters, love. I think I told you once, when you were a small little human, that your grandfather was a farmer. I don't know, you asked, and I gave you the fuzzy shades around the truth. I never talked about my family or my past, and I guess there was a reason. I just tried to make it seem like that was normal, that I wasn't expected to talk about it, and no one would care. Anyway, your granddaddy was a picker. Mostly asparagus, but when that season was over, he'd travel around trying to find other shit to pick. Or, at least, he was supposed to. Most of the shit he picked was bottles of cheap wine and fights with me. I know I told you before that I had only been in a few fights. Well, that's true. It's not a fair fight when it's a boy taking punches from a man.

See, there wasn't anyone there to protect me. My mom died while having me. I don't really know anything about her. I was the firstborn, and the only born. She was the first thing I saw in this world, and for her, I was the last.

So my pop was a mess. He was rough on me, took a lot out on me. He was violent, and I have my share of scars inside and out. Being a kid was hell. Well, not all of the time, but most of it. I was either by myself or in the middle of a shit storm. I spent most of my time trying to slip myself into other families next door or down the block. We lived in a little place on some alley near Grove Street or Depot Street or something. I can't really remember; maybe I don't want to. Anyway, everyone in the neighborhood in those days had their own troubles and humored me, but in the end we are who we are. The one thing I knew and still know is that I wasn't going to be like my dad. And that's the worst conviction, the worst motivation a child can carry.

Honey, you have to know that letting all of this out isn't easy. I've worked through it over the years, sure, but these are things I've always wanted to protect you from. You and Dena and Simon are my little lotus blossoms, my perfect sunshines. I think I did a fucking good job bringing you up, so it's hard for me to expose all the things I've hidden away for so long. You're going to have to bear with me.

So, Walnut Grove. When I was fifteen, something changed my life. I was sitting on the porch of this guy Lee's house down the road from my place with my dad. The day had been steaming hot, muggy as can be. But then the fog started creeping up the delta. It was oozing over the top of the levee up the road, and we sat out on the porch, letting it cool us down. We had the radio on. Lee's uncle had rigged some crazy antennae so that we could try and pick up stations from closer to San Francisco, instead of the Stockton valley crackle we normally got.

The radio was on this crazy station, playing all sorts of blues and rock. A song came on, I'll never forget it. It was "Spoonful" by Howlin' Wolf. I'd never heard a voice or a rhythm or a jangle like that, my sweet baby. It put me in a trance, one I haven't shaken, right to the moment this pen is scratching up this paper. Lee's older sister and another guy's mom from down the street were out there with us, listening. The two ladies were in the same trance I was, I think. They got up and danced on the sidewalk, moving in a beautiful way to this music. They were like some crazy swamp angels, there in the fog, moving their hips and tossing their heads back and forth. The music was running right through them, and it was running through me. It ran through me and filled up all the empty and rotting places. That music saved my life right there, right there on that street in front of all the box-shack bungalows and daisy bushes.

I became obsessed with it. At first, I hitched rides with tomato trucks and equipment salesmen to Stockton or Sacramento, looking for records or trying to see bands play. That went on for about two years after I first heard that magic. Then I started getting restless, wanting more, so I ventured further out to Oakland one day, and it blew my mind. The people and the music and the life. There was life everywhere else in the world all of a sudden. That day I went to Oakland, I lost track of everything in my life at the time and just absorbed, you know?

It got late, and I took the bus and hitchhiked back to Walnut Grove, got in at that time that's almost so late it becomes early. My dad gave me the beating of my life. He used everything he could find in the house when his fists gave out. I'm not even sure he knew it was me he was beating. Didn't matter.

Three swollen recovery days later, I packed my bags and left. For good. It was 1964. I was seventeen years old. When I got on the bus in Lodi, it's like I became a blank tape. Nothing came before, you know? And it was all new material from then on out.

So, Clem, you go to Walnut Grove. I don't want you to see the evil or the heartbreak there. That's all gone now, rotted in on itself. I want you to go there and see the new beginning. Go and prove to me, prove to the universe, that there isn't any hurt there anymore. Know that's where the seed was planted. Know that's where the spirits intervened, gave me motivation.

Love (and oh how I mean it),
Dad

I never knew the pain he had. I never knew any of this. I felt sick to my stomach and quickly folded the letter back up, trying to hide it all away again. This had to be as bad as it could get. This had to be his secret. I called Mom.

"Oh, honey! How are you? I was just reading your email."

"Mom," my voice came out shaky.

"What's wrong, Clem?" Mom sounded nervous, more concerned about me than I thought she would be.

"Um, what do you know about Dad's family? Like, his childhood?"

The line was silent. Mom let out a breath.

"I know everything." She breathed again. "Everything."

"He wants me to go to Walnut Grove next. He told me about his mom dying and his dad and, uh, kind of about his dad hitting him and—"

My mom cut me off.

"Clem. I know. And I hate to say it, but I am guessing that your father didn't tell you the half of it. It's, well . . . it tears you apart, doesn't it?"

"Yeah." That was exactly it. I don't understand how one human being can inflict pain like that on another human being, let alone a father to a son. But when the one being hurt is my dad, my dad who was the sweetest and goofiest and most loving person I ever knew? The details just cut me right in half. Pain and anger.

"I didn't think he'd ever tell you guys about his life then. It got to where it seemed like it never existed. But that's not true. I should have known that."

"He wasn't still stinging from it, though. He wants me to know the history and know why he got himself out of there. He said all the cruelty is gone now." I started crying. For someone who used to only cry from laughing too hard, I was getting a little tired of my own waterworks.

"It is, my baby. It is."

I fell asleep that night on an uncomfortable bed, in a room where everything smelled faintly of bleach, and dreamt of daisies in the fog.

CHAPTER EIGHT

WALNUT GROVE

"Always do whatever's next."

—George Carlin

I left the Comfort Tree and joined the parade of trucks up Highway 99 heading north. Big rigs hauling loads of chickens, new septic tanks, and frozen fast food all rumbled along with me in the mid-morning haze. The golden tan of the dry grass that filled lots along the freeway made it looked hotter outside than it was. I opened the sunroof and let the sun cook the shoulders of my black T-shirt.

Before I'd left LA, some guy in Sunny's apartment complex told me that on the 99, in the dead center midway point of California, CalTrans planted a palm tree and a redwood side by side in the median strip. The redwood to represent Northern California, the palm tree for the south. As I came to the town of Madera, there they were. Almost obscured by the oleanders that filled out the rest of the median, there stood the great California divide. Southern California was behind me, according to the trees. *Southern California stopped at the Grapevine, guys*, I said to the windshield and the trees and the giant billboard asking if I needed legal help for *accidentes*.

This was the longest stretch of highway I'd encountered on the trip so far. One hundred and seventy-some miles. I hopped from the 99 over to the 5 and stopped in Stockton for something to eat and the largest beverage I could locate. I was happily eating a cheeseburger in the parking lot of a drive-thru burger joint when I saw a record store across the street. It was one of the generic chain ones that sold CDs, concert tickets, T-shirts, and even KISS action figures. I finished my food, got out of the car, and jogged over to the record store.

Inside, the fluorescent buzz from the lights was worse than the midday sun outside, so I kept my sunglasses on. I passed the displays for random goth pop punk groups, all black and red and cartoonishly threatening. I was about to reach the "R&B/Blues" section when I recognized something. At the end of one of the aisles, the endless rows of music both beloved and forgotten, was my dad.

I stared at the display. Everything else went away: the bright lights, the over-marketed rap song that bumped through the store's sound system, the two college kids making out in the corner by the DVDs of television shows. I reached out and traced my hand along the edge of his image on the cardboard sign. They had every Condor album and concert video on sale, simply because a heart attack had cut him down too early. I missed him so much more than I thought was possible. All that was left of him were printed pictures and the things he once owned and the letters I held.

I held the edge of the picture of my dad and thought about how badly I wanted to repair him, me, everything. I wanted him to be back. I wanted him to never have felt so hurt. I could feel the cashier giving me the stink eye for staring soulfully at the cardboard figure of a man old enough to be my dad. I would be a little weirded out by me too, if I didn't know. I figured getting tossed out of a record store was not the best plan, so I turned away from my dad and searched the Blues section. F . . . G . . . H . . . There it was. Howlin' Wolf. I wanted to hear the song that flipped Dad's switch, the song that healed him. I found it on a "best of" CD, paid for it, and ran back to the car. I tossed the CD on the passenger seat and got back on the road.

From the 5, I took the exit for Walnut Grove and found my way through the county roads that sliced through fields and traced along the river. The Sacramento-San Joaquin River Delta, clotted by trees and dotted with powerboats, sat just over the ridge of the levee. I put all the windows down and breathed in the air—mud and grass and fish and mock orange and a little gasoline. It smelled like a cheap vacation, and I liked it.

I'd just reached Walnut Grove when my phone rang. I passed the shops and turned into a shaded parking lot as Sunny's chipper voice sang out at me.

"So where are you?"

"Uh, Walnut Grove. You know, up in the Delta."

"Uh, sure. You really are hitting all the California glamour spots. Any revelations in Clovis?"

"Just what I sent you in the email. One former bar, a reformed real estate agent, and that's about it."

"Weird. Anyway, you'll never guess who I saw this morning."

"I have no idea." I was the only car in the lot. I parked in a spot that faced the backyard fence of someone's house and could hear their kids splashing in a wading pool.

"Casey, from that party a couple of weeks ago. I was at the Coffee Bean on Sunset getting an ice blended and there he was, sitting with some chubby girl."

"Hmm. Well, good for him. I would kill for Coffee Bean right now."

"I talked to him, Clem. He was asking about you."

This I doubted.

"I told him about your trip and the letters and stuff, but not too much information. Don't worry. Anyway, he's going to San Francisco this afternoon and he wants you to call him if you make it over there. He says he'll be there for a couple of days, visiting his cousin."

"I'm not calling him, but thanks for telling him my life story. Good one, Sun."

"Aw, come on. I didn't tell him anything heavy. And he's not going to spill it to anyone else. I, uh, also gave him your cell phone number."

"Fucking great, Sunny. Look, I'll call you later. I need to do some stuff here."

"Are you mad, Clem?"

"No, just tired."

I hung up and looked around me at Walnut Grove. I'd demonized it in my head on the way up there, but as I took in the green coziness of it all, I had to admit the town was charming. The main street, River Road, was all shops and cafés on one side, facing out toward the river. Side streets sloped down and away from this, lined with boxy little houses and the occasional picket fence. Everyone seemed to have a porch that overlooked the narrow sidewalks. Trees shaded everything. Down the street, a group of elderly Chinese women waited for a shuttle to come and take them somewhere. Locke, an old Chinese railroad village, was just down the road from here. I'd never been there before but I saw it on the map and remembered learning about it in elementary school.

The place was another time warp. Small and insulated, it had a lazy appeal to it. But I kept thinking about Dad and his life here. No appeal there. I scanned the houses, wondering which was his, all those years ago. He didn't give me an exact address but I figured it couldn't hurt to walk the vague area he mentioned. I mean, he said all the relatives here were long dead. There was a part of me that wanted to come face-to-face with this scar on his psyche. Just being in the town wasn't enough. I wanted to know the motivation.

I walked up and down the streets for a little bit, looking at houses and empty lots and trying to get an idea of what had changed since Dad was here. I headed up the slope to River Road and looked out over the water. It was bright out, a gentle sun, but the water was dark and almost motionless. This was just a sliver off of the Sacramento River, slow-moving water that seeped and escaped from the giant waterway. Islands broke the flow, gave everything a murk. I sat at the top of the levee and thought about Dad.

He protected me. I never knew pain or violence, never knew want or need. I had the exact clothes I wanted, the trips anywhere in the world, the exposure to art and culture, the cars, the meals, the roof over my head. All I ever had was love and support. All those years I complained that I didn't know what I wanted to do (I still didn't), that I couldn't find direction, and Dad never criticized me. He was all motivation, all direction. He saw everything as an adventure or possibility. When I thought I wanted to open a café, he was thrilled and offered to help me get any information or contacts I would need to succeed. He must have known that the idea would be a disaster, what with me not knowing the first thing about food service and not really liking coffee. But he never wanted me to give up on something until I tried it out. And when the café idea fizzled, he said it was because there was something better coming my way, something more perfect that was just for me. I just never really appreciated that enthusiasm and support and I certainly didn't know why he was like that. God, it must have irritated him to hear me complain, but he never did anything but love me more.

"I'm so sorry, Dad."

It was all I could say. All I could say to the reflecting water, to the wisps of clouds, to the trucks and the trees and the rooftops. I was sorry for what he lived through, sorry for his need to hide it away, and once again, sorry for myself.

I walked down the main street, idly looking into the shop fronts and trying to clear my head. "Happiness is an inside job!" came to mind. Happiness was exactly that for my dad. It was something he had to fight for and create and run to. It was an elusive myth he made real.

I came to a small coffee shop and ducked inside. A woman with tight white curls and years on her face smiled a welcome.

"You wouldn't happen to know if there's a family in town by the name of Jasper, would you?" I looked at her, all smiles and held breath.

"No, can't say that I do. Sorry, dear." She smiled back and then pursed her lips until the coral of her lipstick was a feathering seismometer squiggle across her mouth.

"They would have lived here in the fifties and sixties, maybe into the seventies. Does the last name Jasper ring a bell at all?"

"Oh, I've lived here far longer than that and know *everyone* in this town—American, Chinese, Japanese, Mexican, Martian—I know them all." She looked up at the ceiling fan like it could maybe jog her memory. "Nope, I swear to you, honey, I don't know anyone from here with that last name."

I breathed out a thank you and left. I was frustrated, but also relieved. *Thank fucking God*, was all I could think as I walked out of the cool shade of the café and into the bright slap of sun on the sidewalk. *Thank fucking God*. Yet that scab still ached to be picked. I wandered back down the little side streets leading to Grove Street.

When I'd walked by earlier, there hadn't been anyone or anything about save an enormous black-and-white cat lounging in the shade of a bottlebrush bush. Now, though, I noticed an older man walking out to his mailbox. His house was small and neat and had obviously started many years ago as a small cottage and had grown additions like small cancers until it was an imbalanced but well-loved home pushing the edges of its lot line.

The man looked in my direction and nodded and I saw my in.

"Hey, how are you?" I asked.

"Just fine, and you?"

"Pretty good. I am hoping you could help me out with something."

The man turned toward me and softened his expression.

"Oh, lady, I don't have much, and I already give to very specific charities, so . . ."

"Oh, I'm not trying to sell you anything. I just want to know about someone who used to live around here years ago and I'm hoping you can help me. That's all."

"Ah," the man chuckled. "I'm sorry. I've lived here my whole life, though, so it looks like you asked the right fellow. Who are you looking for?"

"A family with the last name of Jasper. They lived here in the fifties and sixties."

The man looked at the ground and thought for a while.

"I am not remembering that name. You know anything else about them?"

"Um, there was a boy, well, man now, about your age. His name was Tommy. His dad was a picker. His mom died in childbirth. I think his dad was kind of, um, abusive?"

"Hmmm . . ."

The man continued to stare at the ground, thinking.

"I remember a couple of families like that. You have to remember that people came and went in those days, especially the pickers and their families. But I do remember one father and son where the mother had passed away in childbirth, but the name wasn't Jasper."

"Do you remember their names?"

"I am pretty sure their last name was Martin. Don't recall the father's first name, but the boy was about my age. His name was John or Joe. Something with a J. His father said he left to join the military or something. Sad story with that family. The mother died, the kid up and left, I think the father said he died in Vietnam. Pretty early on in it, too. Then the father . . . oh, what was his name? Well, he had a problem with the drink and not long after he found out his son was killed in action, he got drunk and drowned in the river. Like I said, sad story. But they weren't called Jasper."

I raised my hand to wave goodbye and he extended his to shake. I held his rough hand in mine and smiled.

"I'm Clem, by the way."

"What a lovely name. Unusual. Name's Lee. It was nice to meet you, Clem."

With that, he let go of my hand and headed back to the shaded front door of his house. I stood frozen on the sidewalk.

Lee. His name was Lee. It was like something electrical gripped everything inside me. I reached into my bag and pulled out the last letter, scanning it until I reached what I knew was there.

When I was fifteen, something changed my life. I was sitting on the porch of this guy Lee's house down the road from my place with my dad.

But Lee didn't know any Tommy Jasper. Lee didn't know any Jaspers at all. For a moment I considered running up to Lee's door, pounding on it and forcing him to read the letter, to remember my dad. He had to remember. Then I quietly put the letter back in my bag and turned to walk away, a sudden sad anger covering me like a heavy blanket. Had my dad's presence here been so insignificant that the people who were such an important part of his creation story didn't even remember him at all? Had he not made an impression on anyone here? If he had stayed, would he have continued to be this nobody, this shadow on memories?

I walked back to my car with so much swimming in my head, I could barely focus.

"He got the fuck out of here and *made* people remember him," I said to no one, to the whitewashed fences and the clumps of cosmos drunk-bobbing in the breeze. "Fuck you, Dad's loser dad, and fuck all of you guys, and fuck this place."

I reached the car and sat in the driver's seat with the door open for a long time. I wanted to leave but I also wanted to make some sort of Jasper's last stand. I unwrapped the Howlin' Wolf CD, fighting with the glue on the security seal, and then put the disc in the car stereo. I pressed forward to track twelve, and there it was.

"Spoonful" wove a spell over me too. I could picture sitting on a porch, listening to the gravel of his voice and the dirt of the guitar and letting it just wash right over me. I could see the women dancing and the fog and the daisies. I could see Dad, and I saw him free. I had a strange sense of wanting to protect him and that freedom. He fought to just exist. and I didn't want anyone to ever take away the sheer weight of that. This place, this sweet little working town that harbored such poison in Dad's father and his actions, may have forgotten him—and good riddance to them for it—but the rest of the world didn't, and never would. Dad won in the end.

I reread Dad's letter and took a deep breath. As I exhaled, I told myself that yes, the evil and the heartbreak and the hurt were gone from here. Cleansed. We were cleansed and everything was blank tape from here on out. I could have a blank tape too. I could start fresh and with some sort of purpose. A purpose to be determined later, I supposed. But an eventual purpose.

I dug around in my bag until I held Letter Five.

Dear Clem,

You made it through some heavy stuff, I hope. I wonder if you are still there while you read this. I also wonder if the place looks different. I'll never know, and that's fine by me. I am in another dimension now, another plane and another reality, so none of that should matter anymore. Well, I hope to be in another dimension when you are reading this. I want to believe that our energy just changes shapes and moves on. What if I am reincarnated as a mechanic in Ohio? Or a corporate asshole on Wall Street? Or a dolphin at Sea World? Would that suck? Who knows. Ha ha!

No matter. Walnut Grove is behind us now. I hope you understand why I wanted you to go there. And I hope you understand why I didn't tell you until now. You figure out what my reasons were, and that will be the answer.

Back when I left Walnut Grove, San Francisco was the answer for me. It warmed the blue skies of my heart when Dena moved there. It's such a great place, such a wild place, and I know that she feels home there. I felt home there too, for a time. I moved there when everything was coming together for me and for society and for music and emotion and love. Age of Aquarius and all that, right?

I arrived in San Francisco with $25 in my pocket. That actually wasn't anything to sniff at back then. I got off the bus and walked over to Market Street and just wow. It was amazing to me. Cold and jumping and free. I stood there gawping at the buildings and the people. Then I realized there was another dude standing next to me, doing the same routine. We started talking, and it turns out he was in the same boat as *me. He came down from Oregon to live where the spirits were filling the air with energy. All he had was a guitar and an address in North Beach where his aunt lived. That guy? None other than Jerald Valone. Yup, Jerry. We walked up to North Beach and I bought us a couple of sandwiches at a deli across from Washington Square Park, and then a couple of drinks at a little bar up the street. From there we couldn't help but take a peek in some of the topless joints along Broadway (Hey! We were teenage boys! What do you expect? Ha ha!). We finally made it to Jerry's aunt's place. She let us crash on her floor, and from that moment on, Jerry and I were best friends.*

We got jobs washing dishes at places like The Gold Spike, and pretty soon we were sharing a place of our own. Jerry wrote beautiful music on his guitar that not only filled up those hungry places in my soul, but also made us a real hit with the ladies. Pretty soon Jerry and I started writing songs together. It was like a dream. We lived and loved and rocked, and it was everything I wanted.

Well, almost everything. I had a job in a bakery for a little while during those years and was coming home in the afternoon after a morning of stacking trays of pastries. Oh my God, they used to make these things that were full of custard that were so good, Jerry would cry. Of course, he always cries when he's been tokin'. Ha ha! Anyway, I walked up to my building on Green Street and there was a goddess on my doorstep. She was staying with her cousin for the summer and needed help getting her suitcase up the stairs. I helped her out, and then that night I took her to the Winterland Ballroom to see Janis Joplin play. Or maybe it was that Grateful Dead/Airplane show at the

Carousel. I don't know. I was too busy grooving on this vision of a woman, this perfect fairy in a long dress that was the color of the ocean at noon. Like I said, this goddess was only supposed to stay for the summer. But she stayed a lot longer than that. As you probably know, that goddess was your mother.

Your mom, my Angie, moved in with me and Jerry not long after that night at the concert. Her family was understandably pissed off. We didn't care. We loved the life we had. We loved the craziness and the electricity of it all. We had a lot of good times in that little apartment and in that great loving city. I didn't know it at the time, but I was building myself, absorbing from everything around me to become a whole new person. I was becoming the person I was always meant to be. There was a reason my life took the course it did. Sometimes, I'm not sure if I know that reason now. But you just have to go with the flow of it all. I went with the flow in San Francisco. I let it wash over and into me. It made me.

The whole time, Jerry and I were writing a lot of songs, but I think the San Francisco scene was just too heavy for us. We tried to find our place, find the moment for us where we could share this music we were making, but it never really clicked. We kept hearing about Los Angeles and how that was the place to be. Jerry left to move down there, scout it out, while your mom and I tried to save up a little more moolah and join him later.

Your mom and I bought that '66 Nova and got ready to leave. We packed the little that we had into the car and then drove around, saying goodbye to the City. We said goodbye to North Beach and Chinatown and the Fillmore and the Haight. Then we drove out to the ocean, just around the Cliff House, and told it we would see it down south. I stood on the beach there, looking out at the horizon's curve, and I felt like the waves on the ocean were the world breathing. I breathed along with it and then thanked whatever is up there for giving me the life and the energy and the brilliance of that moment. Then off to LA.

Next stop for you, my sweetie, is San Francisco. Go see your sister. Go see Washington Square Park. Go see the ocean. Go see Coit Tower and some cable cars. Go see the city. Feel alive and feel in love and know that in every bit of energy you pick up there, a little piece of me is in it.

Love and more love,
El Daddy

I could feel something else in the envelope and turned it upside down in front of me. An old photograph, black and white and cut all wavy around the edges, fell into my lap. It was a picture of my dad. He was standing by the ocean, beneath a sign that said PLAYLAND. He was young and his hair was starting to get long. He wore slope-legged jeans and busted-out tennis shoes and had that twinkling look to his smiling face that always made me feel safe and happy. I flipped the photo over, and in his pencil scrawl was written *Tommy says fare-thee-well to the City by the Bay (San Francisco, 1969).*

San Francisco. I called Dena immediately. It would be so good to see her, to tell her everything I'd felt and seen and read. I wanted to sit with her and have her tell me everything was okay. I wanted her calm to become my calm. I couldn't wait to get to San Francisco.

"Hey, I'm coming to San Francisco today. Shouldn't take me more than a couple of hours to get there. I'm in—"

Dena cut me off.

"Clem, I'm at the airport with Jake and B. I have to go to Portland for an environmental conference, and we're making a little trip of it. My plane leaves in, like, forty minutes."

"Oh." She could have told me about this earlier. She knew I was getting close and she never mentioned anything.

"There's nothing I can do about it. It's been planned for months and I'm chairing all these panels. Shit."

"It's okay. I just really wanted to see you."

"I know! I wanted to see you. Motherfucker! Well, you should stay at my place anyway. I'll call my neighbors and tell them you're picking up the emergency key from them. The Wongs next door. If you're standing in the street, facing my place, they're on the left. Crap, this sucks."

"Yeah, it sucks." I traced my finger along the curve of the dashboard and stared at the fine layer of dust that coated my fingertip.

"So where are you right now?"

"In a parking lot in Walnut Grove."

"Oh, you're really close. Just over the hill from Berkeley. No, wait. That's Walnut Creek. Where's Walnut Grove?"

"In the Delta. Near Lodi, Stockton."

"Huh. So why did Dad have you go there?"

I wiped the dust from my finger onto the thigh of my jeans.

"It's a really long story. Not really one I want to talk about right now."

"Oh, shit. Mom was right?"

"No, no. Not like that. It was just heavy. I'll tell you about it later."

"Okay, but you are kind of freaking me out."

"Don't worry about it." That was Dad's reasoning before. Too late for me. Too late to do anything about any of it.

"Shit, I have to board now. Call me tonight when you're at my place."

I told her I would and hung up. I felt like I was orbiting my life. Me, in a little bubble, seeing everything that added up to Dad and to me but without any way to touch or adjust any of it. Observing it all unfold. What would happen when I got to the center of it all?

I looked up how to get from where I was to San Francisco and started driving once again.

CHAPTER NINE

SAN FRANCISCO

"It is my unbiased opinion that California can and does furnish the best bad things that are available in America."

—Hinton Helper

Getting from the inland valley to San Francisco was a mess. The freeways were jammed but a more frantic jammed than back home. And everything suddenly got confusing around Concord with freeways merging and people cutting over four lanes to get somewhere they were sure of. I just kept trying to follow the signs for San Francisco. A tunnel took me through some hills and dumped me out in the East Bay and right into the most beautiful view of the city. I guess it was the only view of San Francisco like that I'd ever seen since I usually flew in and approached from the south and never got to see it from afar. It was incredible. Everything was luminous, reflective. I crept across the Bay Bridge with all the other drivers and slowly but surely made my way to my sister's place out by the ocean.

Where San Francisco, on approach, had looked all sunshine and radiance, by the time I made it out to Dena's there was nothing but thick fog lurching in off the ocean. I could see it in wisps across the road in front of my car. The sun hadn't set yet, but out here the day was all but over under the thick gray blanket of fog and mist. There was something almost exciting about it almost thrilling the way it swept in and shoved the day away. Dena used to tell me about how the ocean air is full of positive ions and the fog carries them and that's why it's invigorating. Whatever. It was foreign to me and I enjoyed it but I didn't think there was a way I could live with it every day.

I retrieved the keys from Dena's neighbors, a really sweet couple with at least five springer spaniels. Mrs. Wong handed me the key ring, offering belated condolences and an explanation of each key's purpose, as the dogs wound their way around her legs, licking at her hands. She brushed them away absentmindedly with her leg and they went skidding across the hardwood floors, only to come back again for more. As I was talking to her, I felt more and more lonely. No Dena, no one I knew. I was tired from all the driving and had no idea how much more lay ahead. For all I knew, I'd have to head all the way up to the Oregon border before I could make it back home. Mrs. Wong made small talk about the weather and I wondered if she'd miss one of the dogs if I took it. I was getting desperate for company and a dog wouldn't ask me anything. Instead, I thanked her and tried to make Dena's home mine for the night.

I'd figured, before I found out Dena was off eco-lecturing, that I would stay a couple of days in San Francisco. A few days to rest and spend time with my sister and her family, a few days to try and forget everything. Now, though, I wondered what I could do all by myself here. I didn't usually have a problem being alone, but this was different. I was *alone* alone. Normally, if I was by myself, it was because I was avoiding people. There was no one to avoid. Just me, and a San Francisco full of strangers. I'd seen all the tourist stuff there before. I guessed I could walk around, see Dad's old haunts. But then what? Back on the road, putting miles and miles of road behind me again. I just hoped Dena had cable.

Her house was full of *green* appliances and *sustainable* whatnot, all ridiculously expensive. There were wooden or fabric toys all over the place—not a piece of plastic in sight. I wondered if the stuff she bought was really as environmentally conscious as advertised, or if they were just charging more for an illusion of ecological goodwill. The color palette was all sea grass and oatmeal and butter but the random Budweiser fleece throw on the sofa made it all Dena. I laughed as I curled up under it and tried to figure out which button on which remote would bring the television to life.

After three episodes of *Law & Order* in a row, I figured I should get some dinner. I checked out the map for a little bit, then picked through *The Chowhound's Guide to San Francisco* on the coffee table. It looked like as good a time as any to see North Beach from Dad's perspective, so I got in the car and headed downtown. This, I realized as I circled Broadway and Kearny for the fourteenth time, was a huge mistake. There seemed to be one parking place for every nine hundred cars on the road and not a single valet station in sight. I broadened my circles of driving without any luck, but then I spotted a sign on the sidewalk that indicated parking in what looked like a doorway. I got closer and realized it was an alley. I turned in immediately. As I eked down the narrow lane, I saw that the parking lot was actually a courtyard inside the block and was faced in all directions by the back facades of offices and apartments. It was like a hidden little gem. I paid the attendant and headed out into the night.

It was a madhouse on the street. I stopped in the middle of the noise and the motion and the lights and thought about Dad seeing it for the first time. I was sure it looked different back then, but I was also sure the energy was the same. Energy. Suddenly I was sounding like Dena. And like Dad. I walked up the street toward Broadway and Columbus. As exciting as everything felt—the people sitting at sidewalk dining tables, the actual sailors coming out of strip clubs in a blur of back slaps and laughter, the smell of baking pastries and tomatoes and cheese—it made me feel lonely too. I went into a little café that had bar seating with a view of the action on the street and ordered pumpkin ravioli. I took my place next to a bunch of other solo diners and ate in silence, thinking about Dad and Mom and how lucky they were to have found each other in this place. How beautiful that must have been. Mom's fears about the trip seemed so irrational when I thought about how much Dad loved her. But, really, what did I know?

What I knew of Dad or Mom or anyone else was just my perception. What they wanted me to know of them. What little things I'd picked up through the years. It was just like they knew me. They knew a version of me, but I guess I was the only one who really knew myself. And even that was tenuous. Mom's concerns about what Dad wanted to reveal on this trip said it all, really. You could know someone almost all your life. You could share every tiny detail of your existence with that person. You could show them your feats and your faults, lightest and darkest moments, and there would still be that part you just don't know. We all have things we hold back, things that are just ours, things reserved. Did Dad want to expose this part of him now, or was he taking it with him to hide forever? I pushed the last three ravioli around the plate. Holy shit, I missed the time when I felt nothing but vague dissatisfaction. All this analysis was draining. Still, I was kind of ashamed that I'd made it more than a quarter of a century in a state of fuzzy boredom. I paid my bill and walked outside, overwhelmed and exhausted.

I was standing across the street from Jack Kerouac Alley, admiring a mural full of historical San Francisco people I couldn't identify, when my phone rang. I moved back off the sidewalk into a short alcove that seemed to be the entrance to a little dive bar. I pulled my phone from my bag as a group of people leaving the bar walked around me and shot me the odd glare. Fuck them. I didn't recognize the number but answered anyway.

"Is this Clem?"

"Yeah, who's this?"

"It's Casey. Sunny gave me your number. I'm in San Francisco and she said you might be here too?"

Fucking Sunny. I'd forgotten about this.

"Yeah, I am. In San Francisco."

"Sweet. I was wondering if you wanted to get a drink or something."

"Actually, I'm kind of busy tonight."

"Oh, yeah. That's cool. Are you going to be around tomorrow?"

There couldn't be harm in getting a drink with him.

"Sure. I can meet up tomorrow night."

"Awesome. I'll call you tomorrow, then and we'll figure out a place."

Sweet? Cool? Awesome? What was he, a refugee from some eighties juice box commercial? Even so, I was getting tired of being by myself all the time. It had only been a couple of days but I wasn't used to being isolated like this. I preferred to isolate myself on purpose, not by default. I got off the phone and walked further into North Beach, past the square and the big churches, through groups of tourists and young people out on the town. Everything was there to make me feel excited, keyed up. Instead, I walked through the streets feeling shell-shocked. Maybe I really never was able to really feel excitement. Maybe I never felt anything sincere at all. Maybe I've never been anything *but* a blank tape. So when do I press "record"?

The courtyard parking lot where I left my car was silent, the hush a stark contrast to the racket on the street just fifty feet away. I waved to the attendant as I walked toward the corner where I'd parked. A couple was getting out of their car as I passed and as the guy walked over to pay the attendant, I heard the woman with him say, "Nights like this make me happy to just *be*."

Normally, my first instinct would be to roll my eyes, but instead I surprised myself and thought about how lucky she was to feel that way. I guess Dad was finally sinking in. He said to find him in the little bits of energy here. And there he was.

Back at Dena's, I settled in and made myself a cup of very strong, very musty tea. It was all she had and I tried to be open-minded about it, but I wound up dumping it in the sink after a couple of sips. There was an espresso machine on the counter but I was never very good at operating those things, especially one as intricate as this one seemed. I gave up on warm beverages and called Dena to read her the letters and tell her about everything I'd seen. The news of Dad's abusive past left her silent.

"Dena, you still there?"

I heard a sigh on the line before she spoke.

"Jesus, I never would have known."

"I know. What's weird is that I can't believe none of us ever asked him more about his childhood. Isn't that strange, that he told us nothing, and we never asked?"

"Eh, we operate with what we know. The information we have. Sure, we could have asked, but it's not like he would have told."

"I guess. Mom said it was worse than he let on in the letter."

"I don't like to think about that." Dena's voice broke.

"I was pissed that no one there remembered him. You would think that having someone like Dad as your 'native son' would be a big thing, right? But the people I talked to had zero memory of him or his dad. I don't know if that's good or bad, but it still really pissed me off. Dad is someone worth remembering. And I guess I'm also kind of pissed that he didn't let me know about it or think about it. He carried that weight all alone. I wish he would have—"

"What for? What could you have done? He wanted to release that time from his life. He wanted to create something new for himself. Let him have that."

"Yeah, but he still wound up telling me about it in the end. And now we're upset, so what was the point of hiding it?"

"Fuck, Clem. I don't know."

"It all came out in the end anyway, right? What was the point?"

"I told you, I don't know. Let me be the little sister for once. I want to be the one without answers."

"Sorry, Dena."

I could hear the dogs barking next door. This didn't matter to them. Or to the car driving by, or to anyone else.

"It's okay. Listen, this is just heavy and we're closing ourselves off instead of opening up. We need to refocus, Clem. Let's take a minute to be quiet and refocus."

"Oh. Uh, do you want me to hang up?"

"No! We're going to refocus together. Take a deep breath."

I listened to her breathe in while I looked around the room. She exhaled and didn't say anything. I could hear Birch singing something in the background and what might have been a newspaper rustling; Jake reading stories while his wife communed with dead air on a phone line. I wasn't sure how long this was going to go on and figured it would be best to let her talk first. I sat still and waited. There wasn't any sound on the line. I counted to fifty, then sixty. I wondered if she had hung up on me. That would be kind of funny, saying *let's refocus* and then hanging up. I chuckled.

"Clem?"

"Yeah?"

"Did you say something?"

"Nope. Just refocusing."

Dena and I talked for a little while longer. Actually, Dena talked while I wondered if "refocus" was her word for "pretend it didn't happen." I used to be pretty good at pretending things didn't happen. Then Dad died and I got all serious about everything. I didn't know if that was an improvement or not.

* * * * *

The next morning, the hydraulic scream of a garbage truck woke me up to the chill and fog of the day. It was 6:30 a.m. and there I was, wide awake. I got dressed and drank a glass of thick blood orange and carrot juice while I watched the local morning news. I looked out the window and saw Mr. Wong next door coming back from taking the dogs for a walk and figured I should probably get out and get some air as well. I walked the handful of blocks to the ocean and sat on a bench at the edge of the sand. Joggers and dog walkers passed, seagulls played against the wind. The water looked like crumbling gray glass, and I tried to breathe along with the waves that came in but they were too far apart and straining to match the rhythm made me a little lightheaded. But I got the concept. There is some sort of human connection to the sea. There's a human connection to everything, if you think about it. But there's romance in the ocean, longing and adventure and completion. That's what we look for, what we want to connect with. Dad told the ocean he'd see it down south. I wanted to tell it the same thing, but I didn't think it was true. There's too much ocean for it to all be the same. Dad was out there somewhere too. I guess he was everywhere now. Who knows.

I pulled Dad's picture out of my pocket. I'd slept with it propped up against Dena's bedside lamp, figuring that if it made me sad or stressed me out, I could just reach out and turn it over. But Dad grinned out at me all night from that moment almost forty years ago, beaming at me from in front of Playland, wherever that was. I stuck my tongue out at him and put the photo back in my pocket.

I took my time with the ocean, the same ocean that held my dad and his memories. The same ocean that carries winds and storms and goods and people and memories from one side of the world to the other. I took my time, too, heading back to Dena's and getting ready for the day. A long shower, more bad television, some staring out the window at the quiet houses, now emptied for the workday.

After the trouble I had finding a place to park the night before, I decided to take a streetcar downtown. I wanted to wander around San Francisco a little, even if Dena wasn't with me. I caught the N Judah line down the street from Dena's. There didn't seem to be any seats on the train, but then a tiny old woman, a sort of Asian Mrs. Horowitz, waved me over to a spot next to her that she freed up by moving a pink plastic bag off the seat and into her lap. She smiled at me and I felt like maybe being all by myself in this city wasn't going to be that bad. At the next stop, more people got on and some office guy in Dockers stood in the aisle right next to me, his ass kind of in my face.

This wasn't really a problem until he started farting in my direction. At first it just smelled bad. The stench filled the air around us and the old lady next to me made a gagging face. This made me laugh a little. Then, with this guy's ass cheeks just inches from me, he let loose an audible one. The lady next to me said something sort of loud in what I guessed was Chinese. I grimaced and put my hand over my nose. When the guy did it again, I couldn't take it anymore.

"Jesus, man, what is wrong with you?"

The guy turned and looked down at me.

"Wouldn't be a problem if you let me have your seat. Some of us are actually going to work here."

The old woman next to me yelled something at the guy and the train came to a halt. I'd had enough, so I got up and slipped out the back doors. Maybe I wasn't loving this place as much as I'd thought.

I looked around and found that I was a couple of blocks off Haight Street. For Dad's sake, I walked over and figured I would check it out. It was a shopping district, really. Record stores and vegetarian restaurants and places full of used clothing. There seemed to be an equal number of both crusty punks and hippies. Two young guys in black Dickies pants and snug wool sweaters taped fliers for some show on a telephone pole, while blonde sorority girls in search of costumes for their seventies party came out of some vintage place looking disappointed. It was kind of like Hollywood Boulevard, but less coked-out. I walked to the corner of Haight and Ashbury, the famous intersection, the place where I guessed my dad had formed part of who he was. There were tourists in shorts, goose bumped and shivering, taking pictures of the street sign. Behind them? A Ben & Jerry's.

I was tempted to go get a scoop of ice cream but it really was too cold, despite the sun shining down. Instead

I walked up Haight and looked into the shops. I saw a store that specialized in old vinyl records up ahead. I cringed as I approached the window, sure that my dad's face would be there on some album cover or poster. But as I passed, I saw it was just old blues records and some obscure psychedelia. The only face looking out at me was my own reflection in the mirror.

I checked the Haight off my mental list of "Dad places" and headed back down the block to find the streetcar again and go further downtown. When it pulled up and I jumped on, I made sure to stand near the door and not take a seat, even though there were plenty this time. The train jerked its way through what looked like a pretty cruddy area and then dipped underground. I got off at the end of the line, Embarcadero Station.

Up on street level, it was nothing like Dena's neighborhood or the Haight. It was colder and steel gray. Market Street cut a swath through the buildings and there at the end of it, was the bay. I was standing there, being flooded by it all, just as my dad was more than forty years before. I wondered if I was standing in the same place as he was when everything was opened up for him, when he met Jerry and his life changed. It was loud and cold and lonely standing there, but it was magic. I felt connected.

Of course, you can only stand on a street corner feeling "connected" for so long. The moment passed and I decided to wander around a bit. I walked toward the Bay and the big ferry building at the end of the street. I was wearing a denim jacket but I still felt kind of cold, so I walked out into the sunshine that lit the benches along the water. It was still cold there but if I sat with my back to the sun, the fabric of my jacket started to warm up a little, despite the wind. There were boats out on the bay, big sails and little motorboats, all crisscrossing the choppy water. From where I was sitting I could see the bridge, the same one I'd come into the city on, and all the cars racing over it on their way west. The perspective right there on the water's edge was intense. I felt like a tiny part of a picture postcard. All of these landmarks were gigantic around me and it made me feel small and overwhelmed.

I was just getting up to go find something warm to drink when my phone rang. Same number as last night. It was Casey.

"Hey!"

"Hi, Casey."

"What are you up to?"

"Just hanging out. You?"

"Same thing, I guess. You still want to meet up later?"

"Yeah, sure. Where were you thinking of going?"

"My cousin knows some place. Hold on. Where the fuck did he go? Wait, what did you say?"

"I didn't say anything."

"Oh, sorry Clem. I wasn't talking to you. Hang on a sec."

I hate when people do that, call you on the phone but talk to someone else at the same time. I thought about hanging up the phone while I sat there listening to his muffled conversation on the other end of the line but then he came back.

"Sorry about that. There's just all these people over here right now and it's totally crazy. Is it cool if I text you the name and address of the place?"

"That's fine."

"Okay, I'll see you later, then. About eleven?"

"Yeah, eleven."

Here I was feeling so lonely and now I had something to look forward to, some sort of social interaction. It was with this dimwit Casey, but I figured it would be better to go and have a so-so time than to sit back at Dena's and watch television by myself. I needed to talk to people, whether they had bad phone manners or not.

I got up off the bench and wandered toward the ferry building with its event tents sitting outside. It turned out that this was a permanent farmer's market, kind of like the one in LA that I loved so much. Except where the one back home was all food booths and candle shops and stuff, this one seemed like it actually had farmers that brought their produce there to sell. I walked around and checked out the stalls full of fruit and vegetables and the one that seemed to have a million different kinds of handmade cheese. I got a super-gourmet hot dog from a shop and fresh juice from another place and sat on a low cement wall, watching everybody go by.

Mom would love this place, I thought. So I got out my phone and called her. She wasn't home and I got her voice mail on her cell phone. Still, it was good to hear her voice, even if it was just telling me to leave a message. I told her I was still in San Francisco, that I was fine, the city was fine, and that I missed her. I told her that she would love the farmer's market here, and that the trip was going great, and that she had nothing to worry about. I didn't tell her that I was feeling really lonely and that I missed Dad more than anything. I didn't tell her that I was mad at Dena for not being here. I didn't tell her how confused I was or how scared I was of what was coming next, that I was worried I wouldn't understand the point of everything or that Dad was saving the worst parts for last. I didn't tell her that I was tired and sad and just wanted to go home where I could be tired and sad in a more familiar environment. I just told her I would call her later and hung up.

Taking the train down from Dena's was stress enough for one day, so I opted to catch a cab back to her place instead. Flagging one down wasn't easy. I felt like I'd seen thousands of yellow taxis cutting back and forth across the city since I'd been there, but when I wanted one, there wasn't one to be found. I walked back up Market Street, hoping the search would be more fruitful there. Something like eight blocks later, I still hadn't found a taxi, but I did see a hotel. One with a taxi stand out front. I walked into the lobby like I was staying there and then looked around a little for effect. *Shit,* I thought, *if I had known Dena wouldn't be around, I would have stayed here.* The place was nice, and I bet they had a pool. Oh, well. Too late for that. I walked back out to the front and got in the line for taxis that was marked *Hotel Guests Only.* In my head, I concocted a story about my room number or the name under which I was registered, in case the doorman planned to be strict about the guests-only taxi thing. But instead he just asked me where I was going and I told him Dena's address. He blew a whistle, and when a taxi pulled up, he leaned inside and told the driver where to go. I handed the doorman five bucks for the trouble and off I went.

The taxi driver repeated Dena's address back at me and asked for a cross street, just to be sure.

"Outer Sunset, here we come," was all he said. I stared at his handlebar mustache in the rearview mirror and just smiled. The rest of the drive we were both silent, the car filled instead with the classical music the driver had on his stereo. I watched everything go by, watched San Francisco and the people and the buildings. I thought about the woman in the parking garage the night before, the one who was happy to "just be." I wanted that. I wanted that feeling and wondered if I'd ever know it even if I had it.

Back at Dena's, I took a nap and dreamt that I was on a boat in a lake. The boat kept getting stuck on sand bars and I would get more and more frustrated and then the boat would slip free. When I woke up, I thought about how if Sunny had that dream, she'd make me try and figure it out. So I called her to tell her all about it. Taste of her own medicine, I suppose, but I also just wanted to talk to my friend.

"I think it reflects your struggles with the trip. That you keep getting all freaked out but then everything is okay."

"Oh, yeah. You don't think it's just that I sat by the water watching boats for an hour today?"

"No way, man. Dreams are an insight into the inner workings of our minds. Dreams are your mind telling secrets."

"Thank you, coyote trickster. Lay off the peyote, eh?"

"Har har, Clem."

"I'm meeting up with Casey tonight."

"Nice! So he called you?"

"Yeah. I just want to get out, talk to people. I've been alone too long."

"You've been alone for, like, three days."

"Yeah, well, that's a lot. I'm a people person."

This made us both laugh.

"So what are you going to do tonight? Dinner?"

"No, I'm meeting him at some bar at eleven. He sent the address to my phone. I don't know. It might blow."

"Way to stay positive. You complain about being alone, but then you complain about hanging out with people. Chin up, lady."

"I guess."

"Clem, listen to me. You have to figure out what makes you happy and just go there. Stop waiting for the world to make you happy."

"Happiness is an inside job."

"What?"

"I saw it on a pin once."

"Whatever, it's true."

"I think it's also a twelve-step slogan."

"*Eek.* Forget I said that, then."

"What are you up to tonight?"

"I'm going to some art opening. It's that guy Greg's thing. Should be fun."

"Happiness is an inside job, Sunny."

"Fuck off."

"I love you, too."

I felt better after talking to Sunny. I wanted to agree with her, to do what she said and make myself happy. What if that wasn't possible, though? What if I just wasn't meant to be all excited just to *be*?

My phone rang again and I expected it to be Sunny, calling to tell me something she forgot. But instead it was Mom, returning my call from earlier. We chatted for a while about what I'd done that day and San Francisco weather.

"You know the Blaines?" Mom asked me.

"The whats?"

"The Blaines, down the street."

"I don't know who you're talking about."

"You know, that family that moved into the old Ginsky house down the road. The ones who took out all the trees in front and then ripped off the face of the house and put that huge façade on. The house with that enormous door?"

"Oh, yeah. I guess I know who you're talking about."

"Well, I ran into Mrs. Horowitz at the market this morning and she told me that their little boy, Montana, was fooling around at the front door and accidentally shut his hand in it and the door cut three of his fingers off."

"Wait, back up. The kid is named *Montana Blaine*?"

"I know, it sounds like a gay cowboy."

I laughed, especially because it was nice to hear my mom getting sassy again.

"And how did a door cut his finger off?"

"You've seen the size of that thing. It's got to be forty feet tall."

"Uh, way to exaggerate there."

"Well, whatever. It's huge. And it's really heavy wood with a pressed iron front. Lopped those little fingers right off."

"So are they going to get a normal-sized door now?"

"I don't know."

"Were they able to reattach the fingers?"

"I don't know that, either."

"Gee, you and Mrs. Horowitz aren't very good neighborhood investigators."

Mom was quiet.

"Clem, is that what's going to happen to me?"

"Mom, I don't think that our door could cut your fingers off..."

"No, I mean I never thought of myself as defined by your father. Maybe I just didn't want to admit it. But now he's gone and I worry that now I'll just shrivel up into some weird old lady who keeps tabs on the neighbors and listens to a police scanner all night."

"You didn't get a police scanner, did you?"

"No, but you know what I mean."

"I do. But you are your own person, Mom. You have a full life. You do a lot of stuff that doesn't have anything to do with Dad. And the stuff that is related to him and his business is something you created all by yourself and should be really proud of. You don't need to worry about turning into a crazy old lady. You're just fine."

"Yeah. Well, shoot me if I get a cat, okay?"

I watched some television, got dressed, mapped my way to the bar, and got in to the car. The fog around Dena's was as thick as ever and I sat in to the driveway for a while, just letting it blur everything out overhead. Fog is ocean air, pieces of waves made into sky. Dad was in there somewhere. I pulled out of Dena's driveway and slowly made my way back downtown.

I finally found the place, Hemlock Tavern, and parked right down the street. I didn't know if this was somehow good parking karma come my way or an indication that perhaps the availability of a spot was inversely proportionate to the desirability of the locale. Trying not to think about this, I parked the car and went in.

I saw Casey right away, sitting glassy-eyed at a table full of tattooed, shaggy-looking guys in the corner. He got up and met me as I walked in, a bunch of *hey, what's up?* and *yeah, good to see you* between us.

Casey introduced me to his cousin Jack and three of Jack's friends. Casey told me the friends' names but I wasn't sure which one was which. It didn't matter since they weren't paying any attention to us. They weren't outwardly rude or anything, but I got the slight impression that they didn't care for Casey. Jack was on his phone, talking to a friend. The one who I think was named Brady was staring toward the door of the bar, bored with what seemed to be everything. The other two, Carson and Travis, were looking at pictures on a cell phone and laughing, sort of an inside joke thing, I guess. I looked around the place and tried to feel nonchalant. Some Johnny Cash song finished on the jukebox and "The Passenger" by Iggy Pop started up.

We made small talk for a while. I told Casey about driving up from LA. Casey told me about flying up from LA. There didn't seem to be much more for us to talk about. Jack got off the phone and joined our non-conversation in progress.

"So, Clem, you live in LA?"

"Yup." I took a sip of my gin and tonic.

"What do you do there?"

"Uh, nothing." I tried this line deadpan but both Casey and Jack started laughing.

"No, really, what do you do?"

"I don't do anything. Nothing. I just exist."

"Huh. Okay."

I felt a little backed into a corner. I knew these guys all thought that I was just some Los Angeles idiot, someone who could *never* be as hip or ironic or cool as the state that seemed to come naturally to them. I just figured they all had that San Francisco Complex and I didn't feel like justifying their ideas that night. Honestly, I'd never felt comfortable in San Francisco. It's like people there can smell Los Angeles on me and instantly think I'm shallow and undereducated. I just wanted to *be*. Why did it matter what I did? What anyone does?

Casey leaned over to Jack and muttered something in his ear. Jack's eyes got wide and he made a silent "*ohhhh*" with his mouth. This only irritated me more.

Stupid drunk Casey had dropped the Condor bomb. When people found out who my dad was they immediately saw dollar signs. Then they either got irritated with me because somehow they thought *they* deserved the money, at least more than I did, or they thought that since I had this money without working, I should feel obliged to pass it on to them, share the wealth. I tend to stick with people who either understand where I'm coming from or are more hooked up than I am. It's just safer that way.

I started wondering why I'd come there. Why couldn't I be allowed to be some girl in a bar? Not some Los Angeles poseur. Not some rock star's kid. Just a girl in a bar.

Jack's phone rang and he turned away from us to take the call. Casey looked up from the bottle of beer in front of him which, according to Jack, was his sixth.

"Sorry about that. About Jack. Whatever. He's a cool guy, he just didn't know."

"Yeah, it's okay." Maybe I shouldn't have felt so defensive. I thought of that realtor and her pin. *Happiness is an inside job.* I thought it was a crock before but maybe it's the only way to be in charge of anything.

"You know, I saw you." Casey was staring at me.

"Yeah? Well, I've seen you too." I had no idea what he was talking about.

"No, I mean, I saw you out in LA once, but you didn't see me."

"Oh."

"You were at that place, Good Luck, on Sunset or Hillhurst or wherever, sitting at the bar with some guy. You were sitting at the bar, and I saw you as I was walking out, but I didn't say hello."

"Huh . . ." I didn't know what to say to that.

"You were with some guy who had a big star tattooed on his neck . . ." Casey dragged his index finger through a tiny puddle of beer on the tabletop.

"Oh, him. He was a jackass."

"He was on *Jackass*?"

"No. He was *a* jackass."

"Oh," Casey looked back down at his beer. "You think everyone's a jackass, don't you?" He continued to trace his finger back and forth through the spilled booze.

"That's not true at all." I felt like a total asshole.

"Do you think I'm a jackass?" Casey looked up at me, his eyes sleepy and blurred.

"I don't know you well enough to say."

I was being honest, and I tried to make it sound funny when I said it but I think it stung him that I didn't tell him he wasn't. Some girl wearing all black walked in and said hello to everyone at the table, smiling sweetly at Casey and me, even though it was obvious she had no idea who we were. She had a weird glass pendant around her neck that looked like it was supposed to be a fish in a bowl or something. I couldn't stop looking at it. Jack introduced us; I didn't hear her name but I guess she was the sister of one of the guys. Jack and his friends mumbled something to each other, then announced that they were going to head outside to talk to some guy they knew; that they would be back in a second. Casey nodded slowly at them as they walked away.

Half an hour later, it was still just Casey and me at the table. I got up to see if the great meeting of the minds was still taking place but when I got out on the sidewalk, there wasn't a soul around except for the bouncer. I asked if he'd seen four guys and a girl around but he just shrugged and kept staring straight ahead. When I tried to explain the fish necklace to him, he just glared at me. I went back into the bar and found Casey downing what looked to be a shot of bourbon and starting on a fresh bottle of beer. I took the bottle from his hand.

"Casey, I think your cousin may have left. Why don't you give him a call to find out where he is?"

It was getting late, and I wanted to go back to Dena's and get some sleep. I watched as Casey slowly patted at his pockets. Then he reached down and dug through a messenger bag at his feet that seemed to contain his clothes for the trip. Then slowly back to the pockets again. Finally, he gave up and looked at me.

"Fuck, man. I can't find my phone."

He had to be kidding me. I pulled my phone out and called his number but we couldn't hear it ring.

"Well, do you know his number?"

"Not by heart." Casey slurred this out with a half-smile.

"Do you know anyone's number? Anyone who might know how to get a hold of Jack?"

"Let's totally call 911," Casey said and then collapsed into giggles.

"Fine, I'll just drop you off at Jack's house then."

"Okay, but I don't know where he lives."

"What?"

"I don't know, man! He picked me up from the airport and we drove and shit. Fuck me, I don't know." Casey kept laughing but I was getting really annoyed.

"Your stupid fucking cousin ditched you here. What am I supposed to do?"

"I'll just go wherever you're going. It will be fun. We'll have a french fry sleepover." Casey was laughing uncontrollably now and making no sense whatsoever.

I went back out front to see if Jack and his band of San Francisco cool kids had reappeared but it was just the bouncer and a passing transvestite in the thickening fog. I stared out at the streets, all grays and browns in the mist, and tried to relax myself into what this night was becoming. It didn't work. I just felt more irritated and tense. I turned back around to head inside and there was Casey, coming out the door of the bar with a wobble. He smiled and reached out and patted me softly on the shoulder saying, "Condor, I love that shit." I wanted to punch him. I wanted to punch him in the gut and leave him there on the sidewalk for the bouncer to deal with. I wanted to punch him hard and walk away. I stared at him and he suddenly stopped.

"Clem. Clembert. What is Clem short for? Clemmatto. You have to help me. Where the fuck is Jack?" He was pitiful, standing there, abandoned by his own family. I didn't blame Jack, of course. But I also just couldn't leave him there on the street.

"Look. I'll let you come with me but first thing in the morning, you are going to track someone down and get Jack's number and have him pick you up, okay?"

Casey put his arm around me.

"Yes, ma'am. Clemente has spoken." And with that we walked down the block toward my car.

By the time we got to Dena's, Casey was close to passing out. The smell of whiskey or bourbon coming off of him told me that he'd had more than just the six and a half beers at the bar and had probably been drinking for most of the day. He stumbled into the living room and flopped down on the sofa. I got the Budweiser blanket off the chair in the corner of the room and started to tell him where the bathroom was when he patted the cushion next to him on the couch.

"Come here, Roberto Clemente, I need to talk to you."

I just stood in front of him and placed the blanket on his lap.

"The bathroom is down the hall, first door on the right."

"Wait!" He reached out, grabbed my pant legs, and tried to pull me toward him. "I want to talk to you. C'mere, you should totally make out with me right now."

He started laughing again. I pulled my legs out of his grip.

"Get some sleep, jackass." I started back toward Dena's bedroom.

"If you change your mind, you know where I'll be!" he called after me. "You know you want to fuck me, Condor Girl!"

I slammed the door to Dena's bedroom behind me and locked it. I was too angry to sleep so I stretched myself out on Dena's bed and cried instead.

* * * * *

When I woke up the next morning, I thought about climbing out the window in Dena's room. I could get in my car and just drive away, leaving Casey behind. Of course this wouldn't work. But the idea of pretending last night never happened was really appealing. I got up and slowly opened the bedroom door. Silence. I tiptoed down the hall, past the empty bathroom, and peeked around the corner at the sofa. Nobody. Casey was nowhere to be seen. I looked into the kitchen. Nothing. With a sigh, I walked into the bathroom.

It was as I was coming out of the bathroom, tasting Dena's organic toothpaste on my tongue, that I saw Casey on the front step. The front door was open a crack, and I could see his back, his faded denim jacket. He was just sitting there, quiet. Damn.

Despite my earlier inclination toward escape, I figured it would be best to get this all over with. I opened the front door.

"Hey." Casey turned around and looked up at me. He looked surprisingly well for someone so drunk not long ago.

"Clem. Hey, I'm really sorry about last night. I was an asshole. I don't know why I acted like that. But I'm really sorry."

"Yeah," was all I could say.

"I want to make it up to you. What can I do?"

"Try and find your cousin, I guess."

I walked away from him and into the kitchen. Casey got up and followed me.

"Sure, yeah. I just wish there was something I could do to make you not hate me."

"I don't know you well enough to hate you."

"But you know me well enough to think I'm a jackass. Because I am."

Casey fished a calling card out of his wallet and went over to the phone in the living room. I couldn't believe he remembered that part of the conversation last night. He must have remembered everything. No wonder he felt so bad. I poured myself a bowl of cereal and then realized that Dena was out of milk. I looked around for something else to eat but it was all weird pasta stuff and bags of dry couscous. I guess Dena wasn't much of a breakfast person. Casey hung up the phone and came into the kitchen.

"My sister isn't answering her phone. So I can't get Jack's number. I guess I'll just go downtown and figure something out. Or maybe I'll take a cab or something to the airport and try and get a flight home." Casey looked over at the bowl of cereal on the counter. "No milk?"

"Nope."

"I saw a market a couple of blocks down when I was out this morning. I'll go get some." Before I could respond, he was out the front door. I wondered what to do with him. I was such a sucker for redemption. That's why I was still best friends with Sunny. She was always screwing up or hurting my feelings and yet I always let it slide. I always wound up seeing the good parts instead. I didn't need another person like that in my life but I couldn't dismiss the temptation to tell Casey that everything was okay, that what he'd said didn't matter. There were people I've written off before, those who were just complete wastes of space. But there was something about both Casey and Sunny that kind of hooked into me. I didn't know what it was, and I wasn't sure I wanted to. I hadn't even known Casey that long. I guess I felt bad for him. I understood what it feels like to not do anything right.

I got up and went into Dena's bedroom. There, on the dressing table, was my bag. And inside that bag were the last three letters. The market was at least five long blocks away, so I figured I had time to read the next one. Besides, I needed to feel like Dad was with me right then. I wanted some comfort.

Dear sweet Clem,

How is San Francisco treating you? Make sure you get an It's-It before you leave. They make them there, you know. Or at least close to there. Best fucking ice cream treat there is. I'd have them in the house all the time but your mother won't let me. She's always looking out for me. We're the yin-yang. She makes sure I'm grounded, and I remind her to loosen up every now and then.

Speaking of Mama Jasper and the yin and the yang, your next stop is Harmony. "Next stop, Harmony." That's a phrase I love. Maybe I'll use that in something. But you are going to an actual place called Harmony. It's just off the coast on Highway

1. *I've got you driving the 99 and the 1. Because this trip adds up to 100 percent amazing! Ha ha ha!*

Harmony is a little place. I think there can't be more than a dozen people living there. When I say that, I get the image in my head of all these people sitting quietly in a giant egg carton in the middle of a field. Do you see that? Harmony by the dozen? I'm getting a little off track here. I need to back up a little in this storytelling web I'm weaving.

You go through life picking up little pieces of other people. Some of those pieces pass right through your soul, and others stick inside. And other people pick up pieces of you. It's like each of us gives off cosmic soul debris, and we each collect that debris, whether we like it or not. All the debris from my childhood never stuck, because it wasn't meant to. That negativity just washed right through me and I was reborn a brand-new man the moment I set foot in San Francisco. It was there that I started collecting the little bits of people that really matter. Your mom, Jerry, and others.

Sometimes there are people in your life who lodge in you and keep adding and adding and there's no way they will ever leave you. It's important to be aware in those moments, to see the beauty of another person's soul connecting with yours. It's not always pretty, but it's a beautiful truth. And there are times when you are just connecting with the guy standing next to you in line at the bank or the lady in the next car at a stop light. This is humanity speaking on another plane, in other energies, and you can't dismiss that, either. When I tell your mother about this, she always says it's Jung's concept of collective unconscious or spiritus mundi. *But I like to call it The Cosmic Soul Connect. No need making something sound so foreign and old. The Cosmic Soul Connect is now, Mama! Man, I just wrote that out and it really makes me sound old. Ha ha. But you get the picture.*

I've connected with a lot of people and on different levels. We are all human beings in this great big world and we are all in need of a connection. I think I'm really lucky to have connected so fully with the people I did. Life is about a lot of things, and one of them is about taking your place in the fabric of humanity. Share your energy, your soul, and your love.

I knew a guy who knew a guy who owned a little place in Harmony. (That's another great lyric in the making!) The friend of a friend was a glassblower. Now that's a lost art. It's wild to watch too. I want you to go to the glassblowers in Harmony. I want you to go up to the counter and ask for Robert and tell him that you are there to pick something up for Tommy Jasper. Now I, of course, will be dead. Saying this, of course, will freak you out. But I am hoping that at this point you've settled into the rhythm of it all and are not so afraid of the unknown. There's something very important there in Harmony. And you have to be the one to take it in. Get yourself some Harmony, girl. See the energy and the soul and the love.

Love from the ocean's floor to the mountain's peak,
Dad

I sat on the bed, holding the letter to my chest. First, this was the goofy Dad I missed so much. I missed his rambling and his philosophies. I missed him saying embarrassing things and talking nonsense. I missed how he always made sure I knew how much he loved me. Second, there was a part of me that was a little irritated at how timely the letter seemed to be. Dad was right about forgiving and showing humanity and all that. I felt kind of like a shitheel for how upset I'd been. I needed to remember to just go with the flow, to let Dad, wherever he was, help me out a little.

I believed Dad was still with me, that he was somewhere in my soul or whatever. I had to believe that. I hadn't really given it much thought before all this—what happens when we die—but I had always kind of felt that there was just nothing. That when we died, we ended, and that was it. Nothing. I found the other beliefs, of heaven or reincarnation or ghosts or spirits, kind of uncomfortable. But sitting there, I felt like there was no other choice. Dad was out there somewhere and he was still loving me and connected to me. He was going to be with me always. I didn't want to think or worry about what I'd find in Harmony or what I should do about Casey or what all of this meant. I just wanted to hold onto Dad for a little while.

I heard the front door open so I folded the letter back up and went out to the kitchen. Casey put my bowl of dry cereal on the table with the container of milk and sat down.

"Don't you want any?" I asked him.

"I wasn't sure if that was okay or not."

I walked over to the cupboard and got out a bowl and the two boxes of insanely fibrous cereal Dena had and placed them on the table. I went back and got two spoons from the drawer.

"It's okay. Take your pick: Flax Morning or Fruit & Bran."

We sat at the table, crunching away. After a while, Casey looked up from his bowl.

"I'm usually a Frosted Flakes man, myself."

I couldn't help but laugh.

"This really tastes like shit."

"Do you want to go find a coffee place? My treat?"

"Hell yes. There's actually a little place by the beach."

We walked outside and down the street toward the ocean. It was chilly but the fog had burned off and the sun was shining. Casey bought two lattes and two muffins and we sat at a table on the sidewalk.

"So what are we going to do with you?" I asked Casey.

"Well, like I said, I guess I'll just go to the airport. I was supposed to drive down to LA with Jack today. But I guess that's not going to happen. He does stuff like that all the time, leaving people behind."

I took a sip of my latte and picked at the muffin. A fat blueberry fell off the top, rolled across the table, and dropped to the ground. The wind blew it away before I could pick it up.

"I wonder what happened to your cell phone."

"It's probably in Jack's car. I'll get it back from him eventually. So do you know where you're going next?"

"Yeah, actually, I do. I'm going to Harmony. It's somewhere on the coast. I haven't looked it up yet. I hope it's south of here, and not north."

"I know where that is. It's kind of near San Luis Obispo, I think. That's a long drive, Highway 1."

"I guess."

"Are you going there today?"

"I don't have any reason to stay here."

"Could you maybe drop me off at the airport on your way out of town? If it's not too much trouble."

Casey took a drink from his coffee and looked over the top of his paper cup at me. *Humanity.* I suddenly couldn't get the word out of my head and I thought about Dad's letter.

"Actually, do you want to just drive down with me? I could use the company."

"Are you serious?"

"I think so."

"Wow, Clem, thank you. I really appreciate it. Really."

"I know you do. You better."

* * * * *

We got back to Dena's and put our stuff in my car. Casey straightened up the kitchen and the living room while I got directions from San Francisco to Harmony online. We locked up and I went next door to return Dena's keys. When I got in the car, Casey was studying the road atlas.

"Have you ever driven up Highway 1 before?"

"Nope. Have you?"

"Yeah, I drove up to Santa Cruz once on the 1. It's fucking pretty but it takes forever."

"Well, I kind of don't have a choice."

"Oh, I know. You'll like it. It's really scenic."

We headed out of San Francisco and in my head I silently said goodbye to it all, just as Dad did so long ago.

* * * * *

It was nice having someone else in the car. We had the radio on and although the traffic was still clogged up at mid-morning, it seemed okay. Driving this alone had cast a whole different tone to the trip. Sure, Casey was an asshole last night, but he wasn't bad this morning. And having him in the car kept me from being so deep in my own head all the time. Not that I wasn't still dwelling on the letters and missing Dad and worrying about Mom. It just wasn't so *there* in the front of my mind as much. I was finally feeling a little connected to everything. Not fixated or disinterested, but connected.

"Hey, what would you say is your favorite city in the whole world?" Casey asked me this while thumbing through the CD book he found at his feet. "I would have to say Paris. Because it's beautiful, it's full of culture, and it's, well, Paris. Like, everything there looks like *Paris*, you know? And the people are so rude but it's part of the experience. You ever been?"

"Yeah, I went once when I was younger, like eight, and another time a couple of years ago."

"Did you like it?"

"Sure."

"Wow, don't get too excited."

"I hear that a lot."

"So did you think of your favorite yet?"

"Would it be terrible of me to say Los Angeles is my favorite city?"

"Kind of."

"Thanks a lot, Casey. It's just that it's home. And there's everything you could ever want there. You can see anything, eat anything, buy anything, hear anything."

"But it's *LA*. There's more to the world than LA."

"I guess."

"I see your point, though."

"I mean, you don't live in Paris. You live in LA."

"Maybe I should rephrase it, then. Which is your favorite city to *visit*?"

I thought for a moment, tried to think of all the places I'd even been.

"Maybe Bora Bora. I love Tahiti. Or there's another island not too far from there, in the Cook Islands, called Vanuatu. We stayed in this place, Port Vila, and it was gorgeous. Everything was calm, and the water was so blue. That's my favorite place to visit."

"Sounds nice. But you wouldn't want to live there?"

"Nope. Would you want to live in Paris?"

"Maybe. You never know until you try."

"I guess."

We were on the 1 by then, just past Half Moon Bay. We drove on in the fog, getting little glimpses of the water and the rocky coast every couple of minutes. The edge of California was like a gnarled knuckle punch to the ocean here, nothing like the sandy stretches down south. There was no easy drift to the water up here. Too cold. By the time we got through to Santa Cruz, the sun had won out over the fog and everything was sparkling. Casey suggested stopping at the boardwalk, going on rides and shit like that. I just wanted to keep going. We stopped at a gas station and consulted the map. I was sure there was a less precarious and winding way to get to Harmony. We figured it would be better to get the 101 down the road in Salinas and then jump back over to the 1 when it came close to Harmony.

"You've been all over the place, haven't you?"

"What do you mean?"

"You've traveled a lot, like all over the world. Is there anywhere you haven't been that you'd like to go?"

I was usually the one who asked all the questions, or at least just got people to talk. I wasn't used to being the one doing all the talking and I felt a little uncomfortable. I'd rather other people babbled on. But then I suddenly felt really guilty. I was always getting people to talk, but I rarely listened to what they were saying. Was Casey doing what I always did?

"I've never actually been to Salinas."

Casey laughed.

"Well, you're in for a treat. Bora Bora's got nothing on Salinas."

He was right, in a way. While there weren't any sandy beaches or luxury resorts, there were an incredible number of produce trucks. I had barely heard of the place before, but it was bustling. Small, but bustling. It was as good a time as any to stop and eat lunch, stretch the legs, and find a place to pee. I parked the car and we walked around the main street for a little bit. It kind of reminded me of Wasco, but bigger and a little more *with it*. We stopped in a grocery store for something to eat, and while Casey filled a hand basket with soda and juice and what looked like some weird wrap thing from the deli section, I read a laminated sheet on the wall near the entrance:

Salinas: The Salad Bowl of the World!!
What the U.S.A. eats, we grow!
80% of the nation's lettuce
60% of its broccoli
50% of its cauliflower and mushrooms
25% of its celery
90% of its artichokes

I'm not sure why, but the sign made me laugh. They were impressive numbers and all, but it was just so weird to have it coated in plastic and pinned to the wall. Did anyone ever stop to read it? Did everyone here already know all this? I picked up a bag of grapes from the produce section. I had no idea what percentage of grapes came from Salinas, if any, and felt a little bad about that. But I didn't feel like eating celery in the car. I met Casey at the checkout counter and let him pay for lunch. He offered and I just considered it part of his probationary period. I also didn't want to let myself think he really believed any of what he said the night before. I didn't want him to be hanging around just because my dad was famous and I am rich. So if he wanted to shell out $12 on random groceries in some random town, he could be my guest.

We sat in the car in the parking space on Main Street, eating grapes and the potato chips Casey had bought.

"I love this place," he said, after chugging down half a can of Dr. Pepper.

"Really?"

"Sure! It's Steinbeck country, you know. The Salinas Valley. *East of Eden* and all that."

"Oh yeah. *The Red Pony.*"

"That, too." Casey laughed at this, but I didn't know what was funny. I loved that book when I was younger.

"Well, there's also the fact that 90 percent of the artichokes in the country are grown right here." I tried to toss this fact out and stay nonchalant.

"Where'd you read that?"

"Uh, I think everyone knows that. Twenty-five percent of the celery, too."

"You are really strange, Clem."

"I read it on the wall in the market."

"I figured as much. But you also memorized it."

"There wasn't a lot to memorize. I was just trying to be funny, anyway."

"Well, you did a good job." Casey laughed and patted my shoulder.

"I was wondering something, Casey. What do you do for a living?"

"Why?"

"I don't know. Just curious."

"Well, it's not as glamorous as the nothing you do all day. I am an offline captioner."

"A what?"

"I write out the closed captions on TV."

"Like, for deaf people?"

"Deaf people, almost deaf people, lots of people use closed captioning. Bars use it a lot, like when they have the television on but they want to have music on too? Closed captions."

"So do you have to sit somewhere and watch the news and type super fast while people say stuff?"

"Well, no. I don't do live stuff. I can't type *that* fast. I work for a place that mainly does movies for TV. You type out the dialogue, sometimes if there are sounds, stuff like that. The occasional song title."

"That sounds kind of cool."

"Yeah, I like it. Good benefits. And I get to watch a lot of movies."

"So are you on vacation or something right now?"

"You could call it that. I had a couple of days off. Anything else you want to know about me?"

It was usually easier getting people to talk about themselves than this. They usually just talked and I got to sit there, just letting their words run out and all around me. Casey made me feel like he'd seen behind the curtain, that he knew my game.

"Well, if you think of anything, just ask." Casey smiled.

"Okay."

After we gathered up the remnants of lunch, Casey went down the block in search of a trash can. I sat alone in the car and thought more about why I wanted other people to talk, to tell me about themselves. Maybe I wanted them to do all the feeling in life. I liked hearing about other people's emotions but it never seemed like I had any of my own. Maybe that's why this trip was so fucking taxing. I was feeling something for the first time in a long time, maybe ever.

Soon enough, Casey returned and we were back on the highway. He put a Zeppelin CD in, and we only talked in little bits and pieces. A *check that out* with a finger point and an *oh, yeah* of acknowledgement. Casey seemed really relaxed but the more I tried to be that calm, the more I got back to worrying about Dad and the trip and the last letter. What the hell was in Harmony anyway?

CHAPTER TEN

HARMONY

"There's time enough, but none to spare."
—Charles W. Chesnutt

It was a long drive down from Salinas to Paso Robles, where we would pick up the 46 that would take us over to Harmony. It was getting really warm, so I cracked the sunroof a little to circulate some air. When we passed through King City, Casey told me all about how the town was in *East of Eden* and *Of Mice and Men*. I wasn't sure if I'd read either of those. I knew that my dad loved them and had copies in the study. I felt more and more like I had a gap in me, like there was supposed to be all this knowledge about California places and books and history that I just didn't have. I considered myself a Californian more than anything, but I knew so little about the state where I'd grown up. The truth was that I knew very little about a lot. Or I didn't know much about anything.

We turned off the 101 in Paso Robles and started the winding run over the soft coastal hills on Highway 46. It seemed to be all vineyards, as far as I could see. Miles and miles of trellised vines, undulating along the curve of the hills. Casey apparently noticed it too.

"Are those all grapes?" he asked.

"Looks like it. That's a lot of wine."

"Yeah, I don't think they're table grapes. Say, you wouldn't happen to know what percentage of grapes in the lower forty-eight come from this region, do you?"

Somehow he managed to get that one out without sounding like an asshole. It was gentle teasing, sort of like Dad used to do, or Simon, before he became no fun at all.

"You're hilarious. So, are there not any real crops around here anymore? Is it all for wine?"

"Vineyards are probably more profitable."

"Yeah, well, it's these vineyards that are edging us out of complete control of the artichoke market. If we had some 'chokes in here, the cartel would be unbroken!"

Casey laughed then rolled down his window and let the air rushing by gently buffet his hand. He sat up quickly and pointed at a place further up the road.

"Look! It's fucking Hidden Valley Ranch!"

Just ahead, an arching sign was visible at the entrance to a dirt road. The sign said "Hidden Valley Ranch," but I could see how that would be a popular name for a place. Especially one tucked into a valley like this one was. But as we got closer, it really did look like *Hidden Valley Ranch.*

"Is that where the dressing comes from?"

"It totally looks like the label, doesn't it?"

As we drove by, we peered out at the idyllic setting: white farmhouse, rolling green hills, a cow or something.

"God, it does. Weird. What is ranch dressing made of, anyway?"

Casey paused a moment and then put his hand to over his heart and answered, "A proprietary blend of herbs and spices."

"Okay, Colonel Sanders."

"I think it's just buttermilk and—you know what? I have no idea."

"I mean, do you think the recipe is patented?"

"Nah, you can get generic ranch."

This cracked me up.

"I'm not sure why that's so funny but it is. Why is ranch dressing sort of trashy?"

"Is it trashy?"

I felt like such a snob all of a sudden.

"No, I was just—"

"I was fucking with you. Ranch is totally trashy. I think it's because you eat it with other garbage food and they use it to flavor Doritos."

"Garbage food?"

"Yeah, like buffalo wings."

"Isn't it bleu cheese dressing that goes with buffalo wings?"

"Is it?"

"I don't know."

"Yeah, but ranch dressing is trashy. That's been established."

We continued on toward the coast and Casey got tired of flipping through the CD book.

"Hey Clem, you don't have to answer this if you don't want to. But I was just wondering what this whole trip your dad sent you on is for. Like, what do you have to do in each place?"

The reluctance and secrecy I had come to feel as part of me and this trip just wasn't there. I stopped worrying about people knowing or seeing what I, for some reason, kept hidden.

"You know, I don't know what the point is yet. Basically, the letters tell me to go to some city, and my dad tells me a little about what that city had to do with his life. So far, I've really only had to check it out, you know? Just, like, see the place and whatever. They're basically places that were important to my dad at some point."

"So what do you have to see in Harmony?"

"Actually, this is the first time I have to actually go somewhere super-specific. I have to go to some glassblowers and pick something up."

"Maybe it's a bong."

"Uh, okay, Cheech."

"Hey, I'm just trying to help you out."

"Thanks. That was really helpful."

"Sunny said that your mom didn't want you to go."

"What else did Sunny tell you?"

"Just that you had to go on some scavenger hunt and that your mom didn't want you to go. That's about it."

"Well, it's not really a scavenger hunt. Like I said, so far I have to just go see places. My dad just tells me about his life and his ideas on things. I was . . . um, am . . . really close to my dad. He was a really great father. But I am starting to realize that I don't know a whole lot about his story, his life before me. So the letters are teaching me a lot."

"That sounds cool. And what about your mom?"

"Why do you care what my mom has to do with this?"

"Sorry, it's just that Sunny made it sound like your mom was going to disown you for this or something."

"Sunny, as much as I love her and she's my best friend, is full of shit. She doesn't know what she's talking about. Yeah, my mom kind of didn't want me to go. But she just didn't want to hear—never mind."

"You sure?"

"She's worried that my dad had some mistress or secret family out there and that's what this is all leading to."

"Do you think that's possible?"

"I used to think I knew everything about my dad and that my mom knew even more. But now I'm wondering just how much anyone can really know about anyone else. And whether that even matters."

"What do you mean?"

"Well, every single person on this planet thinks they are pretty sure they know who they are."

"Right . . ."

"And almost every single person shares a certain amount with another person or some people. But everything is just what we perceive, right? I mean, I honestly don't know who the fuck I am. So how can anyone else know me? And I can't be alone in not really knowing or understanding my own damned self."

Casey answered me while staring out the window. "No. We don't know anyone or anything. You're right. But the other thing to think about is that no one is just one thing or person."

"Huh?"

"Well, it's like you said, that everything is about perception. People's perceptions of other people change. And our perceptions of ourselves change."

"This is starting to get a little confusing," I laughed.

Casey turned and faced me.

"People change. That's all I'm saying. And sometimes we think we're set out to be one thing and we become another. It's fluid. Us. Everything."

"My dad would have fucking loved you."

We both smiled.

"Hey, what's Clem short for, anyway?"

"You asked me that last night."

"I did?"

"Yes."

Casey cringed. "Oh, God. I guess I did. Sorry."

"It's short for Clementine."

"That's a beautiful name."

"It's an orange."

"Oranges are good. It's also a song."

"Uh, yeah. Sing it and you're walking home."

"Got it."

The hills sloped down then and the air coming in the crack of the sunroof got cooler. The ocean was just over the ridge. Soon enough it was right in front of us and we were on Highway 1. A quick left onto the two-lane road and then another quick left down a little paved street and we were in Harmony.

Harmony isn't so much a town as it is a little collection of buildings. There's a winery up the hill from the cluster of buildings but Harmony proper is just a block long. The sign as you approach says its population is just eighteen. There's a post office and some storefronts and a couple houses, and that's it. We drove to the end of the block and parked the car. It was silent out here. Casey got out and looked at the "Harmony Valley Creamery Association" building that housed the post office. I saw a sign that read "Pacific Glassblowers" in front of a little cottage and went inside.

It was shady and cool in the shop, and it smelled nice, like beeswax and lilacs. I pressed the bell on the counter and waited. It was the exact kind of bell my fifth grade teacher used to have on her desk. She would ring it to signal when time was up on a test. Well, until one day, when she rang the bell and a boy named Nate blurted out, "Pencils down, she's banging her silver tit!" Nate went to the principal's office and the bell went into the desk drawer. After that, the teacher just clapped her hands together loudly and said,

"Okay, time's up!" I think Nate writes television shows for HBO now.

A woman came from a room in the back, all smiles. I was already smiling, remembering the silver tit story. The woman was wearing a denim work shirt and had long gray hair. She seemed really earthy but not in a robust way. Really calm, like she did a lot of yoga and tai chi.

"Hi, can I help you?"

"Uh, yes, I'm looking for Robert."

The woman's face fell a little.

"Oh, my dear, Robert passed away. Five years ago now. I'm his daughter; can I help you?"

"I'm here to pick something up for Tommy Jasper."

We stared at each other and it seemed like nothing was moving forward. The sun was cast red where it came in through the stained glass window in the front and a slice of that red light colored the woman's face, glinted off her long silver earrings. I was about to say something else, I wasn't sure what, when the woman sat down in a chair and began to sob. Like, head on the counter sobbing. I watched the top of her head as she sniffled and cried for a little bit. Then she sat back up and looked at me.

"I'm so sorry. It's just that I can't believe he's gone."

She didn't strike me as a Condork. I got a sinking feeling in my stomach.

"Did you know Tommy Jasper?" I asked the woman.

"Yes, I did. Did you?" She sniffed loudly and pressed the cuff of her shirt under her eyes to sop up the tears.

"I'm his fucking daughter." I couldn't seem to control what came out of my mouth. I was suddenly angry with this woman. Who the hell was she, and why was she weeping over my dad? That was my job, Mom's job.

"Oh my God, you must be Clem. You have your dad's eyes."

"Who are you?"

"You look more like your mom, though."

"What?"

"I'm a friend of your father's."

"What kind of friend?"

The woman's face softened a bit. I clenched my fist in my pocket.

"Honey, don't worry. It wasn't like that. Not that I didn't ever wish it was. I knew your mom and dad from back when they lived in San Francisco. I loved your dad very much, even when he fell in love with your mother. But I always loved your dad even though he wasn't mine. I always wished he'd come around. And then time kept moving on, so I had to, too. But I stayed in touch with him, and we stayed friends. Just old friends." She looked down at the palms of her hands. "I can't believe he's gone. Shit, the pain I feel . . . I can't imagine what you're going through."

"So you know my mom too?"

"Oh yeah. She's incredible. What a wonderful human being. I actually called her a couple of weeks ago. We talked about Tommy and how all you kids are coming along. She was the one, Clem. She was the one who was just perfect for your dad. And he was perfect for her."

"Sorry to—"

"Don't. No need. I get it and it's cool. Listen, you wait here and I'll go get your package."

She got up and went to the back of the place, disappearing into some storage area. I walked over to a stool by the window and sat down. The sun through the window was blue over here, painted across the front of the whitewashed counter. I wanted to dive into it, to fade away into the blue and not come back.

The woman returned holding a large box. She set it on the counter and then came around to the front and stood next to me. She was wearing the same Dansko clogs that Dena always wears. Calm shoes.

"You know how your mom loves roses? Well, my dad used to make the most beautiful glass roses. Tommy was telling my dad once, years and years ago, that he had roses sent to Angie every week. My dad came up with the idea to make glass roses for Angie. Tommy thought that it would be the perfect *big event* gift, you know? So he asked my dad to make fifty of them. He said that he would give them to Angie on their fiftieth wedding anniversary. Or, if he didn't get to see that day, that Angie should get them when he dies. Roses forever for Angie."

The woman reached over and pulled one of the top flaps back on the box, revealing a sea of bubble wrap. On top of it all was an envelope. I'd know Dad's scrawl anywhere and could see that he was the one who'd addressed it: *Angie, my love.* The woman reached under the letter and inside the wrap and pulled out another lump of bubble wrap, this one with a deep red core. Slowly, she peeled away the wrap until a perfect glass rose sat in the palm of her hand. It wasn't some cheesy bobble. It was alive and velvety. Bleeding out pure bliss through its thick glass petals. The color was a deep red, like what it must look like inside us. I took it from her hand and let the light play off of it. Roses forever for Angie.

"I can't believe this. It's stunning."

"My dad was an artist. So was yours."

I handed the rose back to her and watched as she rewrapped it and set it back in the box. She turned to me.

"I'm Grace, by the way."

"Grace who lives in Harmony."

"Yeah, pretty sappy sounding."

"Sorry."

"No, it's a compliment. If only the town and I could always live up to our namesakes. The town does better than I do." She leaned against the counter. "Your dad wasn't like anyone else, Clem. He was such a perfect soul, you know? You're a lucky girl." She was still sort of sniffling.

"Thanks. Thanks for all this."

"Do you want to stay for a little while? I can put some tea on."

"No, thank you. I should get going. Thank you again, for everything."

"No problem, sweetie. No problem."

I picked up the box as Grace held the front door open for me. We smiled goodbye and I left. And there I was. I held the box full of glass roses and stood on the sidewalk, facing the golden hills that hid the sea. This was exhausting. All the creeping suspicions of mine kept getting batted away by

Dad's weird realities. Casey came back from the post office down the block, fists bearing cold cans of soda.

"They were really nice in there. But, I mean, the place is called 'Harmony,' so what do you expect?" He chuckled and handed me a can. We put the box in the trunk and sat on the curb. The sun was getting low and everything was turning a pearly pink.

"Is everything okay? I mean, in there?"

"Oh, yeah. It was actually really sweet. Heavy, but sweet."

"You thought you were going to find something different in there, didn't you?" He looked away from me and out toward the winery up the hill.

"Yeah. I did."

"No secret family?"

"Nope, just a really lovely woman and some beautiful glass roses."

"You can't keep expecting the worst."

"Yeah."

"Hey, listen." Casey put his arm around me in a way that seemed far too conspiratorial and boyish to be romantic. "It's getting late, so don't worry about the next letter. Let's get dinner around here and then we can stay in Morro Bay or something. I get the feeling that any more time on the road and you'll snap."

He was right. So much had happened, and not happened, and I was still processing things that maybe couldn't ever be processed. But I felt like there had been a change; I just couldn't pin it down quite yet.

"You know what? Right now I'm happy to just *be*. Is that weird?"

"That's the fucking goal, Clem."

I meant it. I really meant it and understood it. Whatever came next—another small town, a secret family, empty miles of road, some crazy scandal—I was happy in that moment to just *be*. I think it was the first time I'd ever just let go, and suddenly everything was calm. It just *was*. If this was the point of the trip, the letters, then this was the greatest gift Dad had ever given me.

We got back on the highway and drove down the road a while until we came to Morro Bay. We found a Mexican place that was right on the water and stopped to eat dinner. The place was half full of locals and a few tourists and had a deck that looked out over the ocean. The sun was going down and I was content and relaxed, sitting there on the edge of the world.

We ate enchiladas and shrimp and made our way through a couple pitchers of margaritas, talking about nothing at all, really. I kept taking deep breaths, feeling like each exhale erased more and more of my stupid worries and complaints. I was on the beginning of my blank tape and I didn't have any fear of what kind of track I'd lay down. All that mattered was that it was new and blank and mine.

"If you had to pick one all-time, greatest song ever, what would it be?" Casey asked me.

"Do you have a list somewhere of things you ask to stimulate conversation?"

"What do you mean?"

"The first time I ever talked to you, you asked me what the worst thing I'd ever done was. Which, by the way, was a little strange and kind of inappropriate. At that bar in San Francisco, you asked me what I thought the three most important inventions were. Now you want the best song ever. I just think it's funny."

"No, I don't have a list somewhere. I'm just curious."

We sat there quietly for a while. A seagull landed on the railing of the deck and strolled nonchalantly toward a recently vacated table until a busboy came over and swatted at it with a rag.

"'Summertime Rolls.'"

"Huh?" Casey looked at me.

"'Summertime Rolls' by Jane's Addiction is my vote for best song ever."

Casey smiled at me.

"See? You couldn't resist my genius brain and its fascinating question. So why is that the best song?"

"I don't know. It makes me feel nostalgic. A little melancholy, but in a good way. The words are sweet but not stupid. The music is beautiful, really gorgeous. I don't know. Describing music never does it justice. I just like it. I never get tired of hearing it."

Casey nodded along with what I said while he pushed what was left of some rice around on his plate.

"So what's your favorite?"

"Lately, I'd say Neil Young's 'Harvest Moon' is my favorite, because of the guitar in it being so gentle and the words just, I don't know. It's like the nostalgia thing you were talking about. The song makes me think of being young and outside at night under the stars. It's like it created an invented memory for me. I like that."

This was a long way from the guy who beat someone to a pulp at Dodger Stadium or the drunk asshole I hated so badly last night. Maybe he wasn't so bad to have around. Annoying, yes. But I think he just wanted people to like him, wanted to feel connected. Kind of like me. Kind of like anyone, really.

"Can I ask you something about that Dodger Stadium incident of yours?" I asked. "You don't have to answer if it's uncomfortable or anything."

"I guess. What do you want to know?"

"Um, you said you just sort of snapped when you beat that guy up and that you aren't violent . . ."

"Don't worry, Clem, I am totally not a violent person. You don't have to worry."

"Oh, no. I believe you. I was just wondering if you saw or, um, experienced violence in your childhood."

"You want to know if I was abused?"

"No, well . . . just . . . maybe I shouldn't have asked."

"It's okay. Here's the deal: My dad was a drunken asshole. He never hit me, and he never hit my mom, but he had these . . . outbursts. He broke a lot of shit in the house when he'd get mad or drunk or both. I learned later that my mom felt like I did, that if we pushed him, we would be next. We would wind up like the wall in the den or the picture frames or the platter in the kitchen."

"Oh . . ."

"He left us on Christmas Eve when I was eight. He started screaming at my mom and I hid behind the sofa in the living room. He just wouldn't shut up and my mom was crying and that just made him angrier. Then he just picked up the whole fucking Christmas tree, carried it over to the sliding glass door that led out to the patio, and threw the tree outside. He came back into the room, stomped on the presents, and then walked out. I never saw him again."

"Holy shit."

"I think it saved our lives, him leaving. But it's weird that you asked me about seeing violence as a kid and that whole Dodgers thing. When all that went down and I got home, I was just standing in my bathroom, staring at the mirror, and getting so mad because I was turning into my dad. I was disgusted. I felt fucking dirty, you know? So every single day, I tell myself I am not ever going to be him. Yeah, I drink. But not like he did. I am just not going to be that angry, mean person. I am going to be me. My own me."

"I am so sorry."

"Me too. Especially for my mom. But we wound up okay." Casey looked out at the ocean and then back at me. "What made you ask?"

I felt so open and fearless that I decided to share with this practical stranger a pain my dad had kept hidden his whole life. But I felt like the more I talked about it, the less power it would have.

"You seem like a really insightful and caring person. I mean, you have your weird drunken moments, but we all do, I guess."

We both sort of chuckled and I continued. "My dad had me go to the town where he grew up, Walnut Grove. What's kind of crazy is that I never really knew anything at all about his childhood. Nothing. And I didn't ever really ask. Anyway, his letter told me all about how *his* dad used to beat the shit out of him on a regular basis. And so my dad ran off and left that all behind. He was . . . he was the kindest and gentlest person I've ever known, will ever know. And I guess I just have trouble understanding how he survived what he did and how he didn't carry it forward. So I wondered if you had that in your past, and how you shook it."

"Your dad probably had one of those moments where he looked in the mirror and knew he couldn't be his old man. Just like I did. You either break the cycle or you ride it on into your own created hell."

"You're a good man to see that, Casey."

"And you are a really lucky woman to have had such a good father. Seriously, I can tell you what not having a dad around does. It eats away at small things that fuck with you in weird ways. You were really lucky."

"I know. And I'm seeing that more and more now."

* * * * *

We paid the check and then drove down the road a little bit until we found a motel with a vacancy sign. The place was hanging on tight to the sixties California beach look, all faded blues and mod archways, but it looked clean and that's all I cared about. The woman at the front desk was filing her nails as we walked in.

"Can I help you?"

"Yeah, we'd like a room, please. One night." As soon as I said it, I realized it sounded sort of illicit and this made me start laughing.

"We only have one left. It's got two double beds. Is that okay with you two?"

This made me laugh even more. Casey just looked at the tops of his shoes.

"Actually, that's perfect. We'll take it."

"Okay, that's $135. I know the sign outside says 'Free HBO,' but the cable's on the blink, so there's no HBO. Check-out is at 11:00 a.m. And we don't take American Express."

I handed her my credit card while Casey went out to the car to get our bags.

"Your boyfriend's pretty quiet."

I was going to correct her but then figured it didn't matter anyway. "He's just shy."

She handed me the room key and went back to filing her nails.

The room was up a set of concrete stairs and at the very end of a very long open-air corridor. We settled in and I hoped Casey would come up with another one of his stupid conversation questions because I wanted to know more, and, oddly, to tell more.

"So, uh, how's that bed treating you?" Casey was reclining with his back against the headboard. He flipped back and forth between the only two channels on the television and then shut the whole thing off.

"Bed's great. Thanks for asking." The margaritas from dinner still made me feel soupy and warm. "C'mere," I said. "See for yourself." The words came out before I could stop them.

Casey got up and flopped down next to me on my bed. We both had our heads on one of the starched, papery pillows and were staring at the blank TV screen. I listened to him breathe right there beside me and thought about what he said last night, whether that mattered. He still had the remote in his hand and switched the television back on, this time to a channel that was nothing but static. He sighed and turned the set off.

He raised the remote again and was about the turn the power back on when I reached over and grabbed his hand.

"Stop," I laughed.

I held him by the wrist and for a little while we just stared at each other. He flicked the remote out of his hand, toward the other bed, and then leaned into me. I was still holding his wrist and now our faces were inches away from each other. I could smell the tequila on his breath and the warm cinnamon of the red disk of candy he'd grabbed from the bowl on the way out of the restaurant. He pulled his wrist toward his mouth, taking my hand with it, and then kissed the tips of each of my fingers. I couldn't help but giggle and this made him laugh too.

"So suave," I told him.

He laughed again and looked down at the bedspread. I looked down at it too; it was rust colored with a faint green fleur-de-lis design running the length. It was horrible and made me laugh even more. Casey leaned in, for real this time, and we kissed. We kissed, and I didn't want to laugh. I wanted to keep kissing him so that feeling of warmth and happiness like yellow rays on water would keep swimming around me forever. We kissed, and his fingers were in my hair, tracing the line of my collarbone. We kissed, and I tugged at the belt loop on his pants, held his lower lip between my teeth.

He leaned further over and was on top of me then. I was running my hand under his T-shirt and he shifted. I could feel him hard against my hip. We stopped, looked at each other, and laughed again.

"I really like you, Clem."

He started to take my shirt off but I stopped him.

"Wait." I didn't want him to make this into anything other than us messing around in a motel room. But I didn't know how to say that without sounding like, I don't know, Sunny.

"What's wrong?"

"Nothing, uh . . ."

"Is this about last night? What I said?"

"No. I just—I don't have any condoms."

Casey reached into his pocket and pulled out a cardboard square, opened it up, and produced a silver foil condom packet.

"Where did you get that?"

"From the vending machine in the bathroom at the restaurant. Classy place, huh?"

"That was presumptuous of you."

"Hey, be prepared, right?"

I was looking at him, looking at the little scar on his cheekbone and his mossy green eyes.

"Yeah, be prepared."

"I was going to tell you that I really like you. And I'm sorry if I hurt your feelings before. That isn't who I am."

I tried to tell myself that I just wanted to get outside myself by fucking him, an entertaining distraction. But he was so sincere and I had to acknowledge that I did like being around him. I did like sharing things and letting him in.

I pulled his shirt up over his head and tossed it on the floor. I could hear the ocean or the freeway outside, I couldn't tell which. I had my shirt off then and the click of him unbuckling his belt became everything in the room.

CHAPTER ELEVEN

"A high station in life is earned by the gallantry with which appalling experiences are survived with grace."

—Tennessee Williams

Casey was still asleep when I woke up so I showered, got dressed in a pair of dark green cords and a shirt with little blue birds all over it, and sat on the other, still-made bed and answered some emails. I told Mom I was in Morro Bay. I thanked Dena for letting me stay at her place and told her the keys were back with the neighbors. I told Simon about the roses but asked him not to tell Mom yet because I wanted it to be a surprise. I started an email to Sunny, telling her what an asshole Casey had been back in San Francisco but that I'd slept with him anyway last night. I deleted that draft and shut everything down. I looked over at Casey and wasn't sure what to think.

I wasn't giddy about *him*, but I was giddy. I was filled with the
excitement of what could come next. This was the beginning
of my own tape, my own trip, and I had to admit that this
was all pretty fucking exciting.

I got my bag and pulled out the last two letters. The more
Dad showed me, the more he gave away, and soon there
wouldn't be anything new. No new conversations with him,
no new information. It's easy to think you should embrace
the unknown if you feel like one day it won't be unknown
anymore. I felt like that would be true for me someday, so I
opened Letter Seven.

My darling Clementine,

*I hope you were able to take care of the business in Harmony.
I bet you are having a blast with this, all the learning and
seeing and traveling around. As much as I wish I could have
gone along with you on all this (in a way I am, of course), I am
glad you are able to do this on your own.*

*When your mom and I moved to Los Angeles, it wasn't the
bowl of sweet cherries I thought it would be at first. We struggled
to find a place to live, to find ways to make money, to feel like
we belonged. People come from all over the world, from every
corner of the planet, to try and make it in LA. It's a brave move
to accept your dreams as a map and run with it. I know it's easy
to criticize the kids who get off the bus each day from the middle
of nowhere, hoping to be rich and famous, but I respect them. I
was them. People talk about how these kids don't have talent,
just a desire to be a celebrity. Well, I think drive* is *a talent. And
as much as I like to talk about how I was writing songs and*

feeling the music, when I first got to Los Angeles, I didn't have a whole lot of talent in my soul. But I knew that I was destined to be something, and there was no avoiding that.

I wrote "Loving Rose," and Jerry said it was amazing. He'd met up with some other guys and we formed Condor based pretty much on that song and the fact that we all wanted to rock. But "Loving Rose" isn't really a rock song. And it's only one song. So I got to work writing some other stuff while the guys jammed and let the spirit of the music move them.

I stayed up for days, trying to come up with ideas for songs, but nothing came. I was working at a dry cleaners and your mom got a gig as a secretary for some insurance office. We worked all day and at night I tried to write songs and your mom took community college classes. This, my baby girl, was the time of No Fun. It seemed like the harder I tried to spill my heart and soul onto the page, to sing it out for the world to hear, the less came out of me. It was frustrating and, to be honest, I wondered if it all wasn't a big mistake. I wondered if maybe I should have just gone and picked up some company job and ignored the music in my head and in my soul.

Jerry told me to just relax and let the words come. He and the guys were writing some fucking righteous tunes and he said that when I was ready we'd have magic on our hands. So I started to just look around me and try writing what I saw every day. I looked at the clouds in the sky and the people who came in to pick up their clothes at the cleaners and the birds on the fences and the buses in the street. I put down the details and finally wrote a song.

I took it to the guys and read it out to them. I called the song "Boat Show Woman." Hey, I'm embarrassed about that today but at the time I thought it was great. I thought I was really capturing something there, really tapping into a reality. So I read the guys the lyrics and they were silent. I tried singing the lyrics to one of the tunes they'd created. "Boat show woman, with your yellow dress, you are such a mess, give it to me . . ." The guys stayed silent. Ha ha! Holy shit, I don't blame them. That was pretty much my low point right there. I used to want to go back in time and erase it but I can't, and now I don't want to. Anyway, Jerry wouldn't look at me. Rick told me I was bullshit. I walked out of the practice pad and sat in the car. I was broken. I worked so hard and came up with crap. Finally, Jerry came outside and explained to me that I was missing the mark. I had to look into the face of the music, the face of God, and report back what I saw.

I went back inside and listened to the guys play for a while and then I went home. I told your mother about what happened and she didn't see me as some loser who wrote an idiotic song. She loved me for the man I was and told me to just let the words come to me, that even if it didn't work out with the band, she still believed in me. She thought—no, she KNEW—that I was worth something, and she got me to see that too. I got back to work and let that music flow right through me, just like I did back in Walnut Grove. I let the music tell the stories. I let the music guide me. I wrote some great stuff and went back to the band, and they were a little more receptive.

Sometimes, Clem, the ship goes down. But that doesn't mean the end. You have to fuck up royally sometimes in order to get it right. I've made a lot of mistakes in my life but those mistakes were mine alone. Sometimes they were even too big to be called mistakes. But I always made it right. I stayed true to what was important in life. Goodness and music were my masters and I never strayed. It's okay, honey, to stumble and fall. You just have to make sure you make it right. Los Angeles was all failure for me at first, it was making me think that maybe I couldn't just start from scratch, that I wasn't meant for something better. But as I picked myself back up, it became all beauty for me and I never stopped working to always make things right.

Los Angeles is family. It is creativity. It is home. Go home, baby. Go back to Los Angeles and don't ever forget that you can always start again. Don't forget that there's always redemption and there's always a place to call home.

Warmth from my heart,

Dad

Dad seemed to almost be admitting something but I didn't have a clue what that something might be. Did it even matter? Everybody's got to have somewhere to go, someone who will always love you no matter how bad you fuck up. That's what family is all about. Loving unconditionally. Did I think that Dad ever cheated on Mom? Was that what he had to make right? That wasn't any of my business, really. All I had to do was love them both no matter what, and that was easy.

* * * * *

Casey woke up and greeted me with a smile and sleepy eyes like you'd say good morning to a friend, which was a relief. I didn't want him to be all weird. We still had another couple of hundred miles to go. But at least I was going home.

He took a quick shower and I got my stuff together to put in the car. I didn't bother mapping the way back, just figured I'd take 1 or the 101 until I knew where I was. I thought I'd probably drop Casey off wherever it was he lived and then go to Mom's and give her the roses. I really hoped that Casey didn't live in Huntington Beach or something. I didn't want to have to drive all over the place, be so close and yet so far from home, you know?

We checked out of the motel and had breakfast in Morro Bay. The day was so clear that it felt like I could see the curve of the earth as the Pacific spread out on the horizon. It was warm and still and bright. I was feeling better about everything, glad to be going back to LA, but also a little sad that the trip was almost over. I wouldn't miss the worry and anxiety which I still had because there was still that last letter and I knew Dad would save the big one for last. But I would miss the excitement of a new letter, a new town, a new way to look at things.

We drove along, waves breaking on the right, strawberry pickers hunched over the crop on our left. I thought about that warden in Wasco, about his grandfather picking strawberries. Then I thought about the grandfather I never met, picking asparagus. I was glad I never knew him. I pulled my attention back to the road when a big black pickup truck loaded up with surfboards passed us and the red convertible in front of us in one aggressive leap.

"What the . . ." Casey looked intently at the truck.

"Dude, I don't care if he passes me. I'm not speeding up."

"No, look down there." Casey pointed to the area just below the truck's rear license plate. There, swinging from the bottom of the truck's fender, were big pink balls.

"Oh, God."

"What the fuck is that? Is that a nut sack?"

"They're called Bumper Nuts."

"What?"

"Bumper Nuts."

"And you know this because . . ."

"I heard that they sell them at truck stops. They come in silver too."

"That's kind of gross."

"Yeah. I think it's kind of funny, though."

"I wouldn't put them on my car."

"Neither would I, but at least it's something to look at on the road. Believe me, you drive all day, you start to appreciate the little things."

"I can see that."

"Like I started to notice that the more shit people had in their back windows or hanging from their rearview mirrors, the worse drivers they were."

"Huh."

"It's true. Start watching for it and you'll see. It's the people with dozens of stuffed animals in their back windows or the ones with, like, fifty strands of beads and a graduation tassel and three parking passes hanging from the rearview. They can't see out of the windows but they also just make idiotic driving maneuvers. And what's with the tissue boxes in the rear window?"

"Tissue boxes?"

"Seriously, you have no idea how many people have tissue boxes on the ledge above the backseat. It's not like they can reach it while they're driving. Do they have lots of passengers with allergies?"

"I like the people with those deodorizing crowns in the back window."

"Oh, I know those."

"Have you ever smelled one? Fucking disgusting."

"You know who else are bad drivers? Men in minivans. They drive all crazy. I think they're pissed off at being emasculated by their own cars."

"Then they should get those Bumper Nuts to even it out."

"Ha ha. Maybe. Give them balls to ease the driving aggression."

"It's like how getting a dog fixed calms them down, but in reverse."

We lost sight of the truck after it sped up to pass the red convertible. We stayed behind the car with its top down and drove along, chatting and laughing about bad driving indicators. Casey looked through the CD book and picked a disc, Elliott Smith. We listened and drove, making good time but staying at a relaxed pace. It was nice. We were further inland then, beyond San Luis Obispo, and surrounded by golden rolling hills. Those California hills always look so soft from a distance, like lumps of mustardy velvet. Even when they're green or covered in oaks, you get the notion that touching them would be like patting puffs of cotton. But then you realize that up close they are probably hard and covered in scrub, all brittle grass and stones. When you look at them from a distance though, when you see them from a passing car or out a window, they look like honeyed heaven.

We had the sunroof open and the heat of the sun on my arms felt good, even though I knew I'd probably be burnt later. We briefly discussed stopping in Solvang, that weird Swedish or whatever it was town, but figured it would be best to keep going. We were getting closer to the ocean again and I was eager to get home. The stereo played "Can't Make a Sound" as we floated on the highway, everything whipping by us in a flowing blur.

I listened to the lyrics and thought about my dad writing songs. How the hell did he come up with things? How did he get his ideas into words that made sense? I chuckled a little to myself remembering his "Boat Show Woman" song. Casey reached his arms up and stretched through the sunroof. Everything felt calm and lazy, so different from my drive north.

"Hey, do you . . ."

I suddenly forgot what I was going to say.

"What's that?"

"Never mind. I forgot. Means it wasn't very important anyway."

"Okay."

"I love this song."

"More than 'Summertime Rolls'?"

"Maybe I can like more than one thing best."

"Maybe you can. Maybe we all should."

Ahead of us, the red convertible was about to round the turn in the road when some big, nondescript sedan came screeching around in the opposite direction. Whoever was driving must have been going too fast for the turn and had to overcorrect, but this move put the car in our lane, coming right at us.

The sedan hit the convertible head on, their headlights smashing together. The noise was incredible, enough to make me jump a little in my seat. The convertible immediately began to spin out toward the right shoulder, while the other car flipped over and continued on its path, heading directly for us. I slammed on the brakes and jerked the car onto the gravel shoulder just as the sedan whizzed by us, covering the pavement we'd just occupied in a shower of sparks and broken glass. I could feel the wind and the heat as it whipped by but I was too scared to look and just stared straight ahead. Stared ahead at the passenger of the convertible as he floated out of the car like a toy, like a dropped sock. He landed in the brush while the convertible spun and skidded to a stop just beyond the turn in the road. My car stopped, dust rising around us like a bad smoke machine, the stereo still blaring.

I jammed my finger at the volume button and shut off the music so that all there was in the air was the dust and our panicked breathing.

"Are you okay?"

I turned to look at Casey. He was staring ahead at the guy in the bushes and didn't answer me.

"Casey, are you okay?"

He looked over at me finally.

"I'm fucking freaking out. Holy shit . . ."

"I know."

"Holy shit. Holy shit . . ." He just kept saying that and looking out the window.

"We've got to see if they're okay."

I got out of the car and looked behind me. The sedan was upside down in the middle of the road, the driver moving just a little as he hung upside down in his seat. I turned back toward the convertible. The front of the car was a mangled mess, shooting steam up at the blue sky. I started jogging toward it, hoping that whoever was driving was still alive. I turned to see Casey heading toward the upside-down sedan. The driver of the first car to come upon the whole mess was standing with his arm on the top of his open car door, a cell phone stuck to his ear.

Everything went from insanely loud to freaky quiet and all I could do was focus on the sound of my shoes on the roadway. I could see the convertible passenger's khaki pant legs in the brush up ahead and I took a deep breath before diverting from my jog to the convertible to check on him. He wasn't wearing shoes which I thought was weird, but then I saw his deck shoes in the grass a little further away and figured he'd been knocked right out of them in the impact or whatever. I didn't have to get closer than fifteen feet from the guy to see that he was dead. His neck was snapped, putting his head at an unnatural angle, and there was blood coming out of his mouth and his ears. His eyes were wide open. I stared at him and wished that I'd never seen him like that, that I could erase this moment from my mind. But the more I wished it gone, the more the image burned into me. I looked back at Casey again. He was kneeling in the road at the window of the sedan and seemed to be talking to the driver. He looked up and over at me. I shook my head at him. He knew I meant that the guy was dead and he just looked down at the pavement for a second then went back to talking to the sedan driver who still hung like a bat in his car.

I turned toward the convertible. As I got closer, I could see the driver was a woman in her thirties or forties. She was still buckled in and was slumped against the door. I thought her radio was still on too, but when I got next to the car, I realized it was her talking. She was mumbling a bunch of gibberish, an odd droning buzz. I reached over and put my hand on her shoulder. The fabric on her shirt was wet but I didn't know why.

"Hey, are you okay?"

I didn't know what else to say to her. I mean, she obviously wasn't.

"I said fourteen and framing blocks there were blue and green but how you go . . ."

Not okay.

"Um, ma'am? Can you tell me your name?"

She looked up at me when I asked her this. A cut on her head where her hairline met her forehead sent blood down her face in little jagged rivulets. Her bottom lip was swollen and I could see the bite marks, two little dashes, where she'd bitten through it. Her teeth were covered in blood and spit and I wished I had some sort of cloth or something to help her clean up, but where would I start?

"I'm Maureen."

"Maureen, my name is Clem. You had an accident and we're getting help right now, so just hang in there, okay?"

Maureen looked at me and raised her eyebrows. It was like she couldn't see anything around her until I said that. She looked at my face for a while and then slowly turned and took in the chaos and destruction around her. She looked down at her legs and I couldn't help but follow her gaze. It was apparent that she was stuck pretty good in what was left of her car.

"I can't move my legs. I think I'm stuck."

I gently patted her shoulder again, hoping I wasn't hurting her more in my effort to comfort her.

"I know, it's okay. Help is on the way. You're going to be fine."

I hoped I was right. In front of us, cars were starting to back up on the highway but no one was getting out to help. People either just sat in their cars or stood next to them, watching from afar and calling for help on their phones.

Maureen slowly turned her head and shoulders to her right, toward the empty seat beside her.

"Where's Leo?"

"Um, Maureen, help is on the way. Just stay calm."

"Where's Leo?" She was starting to panic. I didn't know what to tell her.

"Maureen, it's okay, just stay calm."

She tried to unbuckle her seatbelt but in her fumbling got woozy and started spitting up blood. I reached out and held her down in the car seat.

"You need to stay calm. Look at me. . . . Look at me."

Her eyes didn't seem to be focusing and she was starting to babble again.

"I can't die! There's not enough time! Where's Leo? God, there's not enough time!"

I could hear sirens approaching and turned to see a CHP cruiser and a fire truck weaving their way through the traffic that had backed up behind us. Casey was standing with the guy who had originally called for help. They stood with their arms crossed and watched as the fire truck pulled up next to the overturned sedan. Firefighters with all sorts of gear spilled out of the truck and made their way to the car. One of them put on latex gloves and then bent over to talk to the driver. I looked at my own hands. No blood.

Two more highway patrol cars and an ambulance came from the road ahead of us, edging their way through the maze of onlookers. I could hear more sirens in the distance, more people coming to help. Maureen was crying, looking over at the empty passenger seat.

EMTs ran up and started tending to Maureen, and as some highway patrol officer walked me back to my car, I could hear her screaming behind me.

"No! There's not enough time!"

There were flares all over the roadway now, everything marked off and secure. Everything in a state of suspended calamity—the car upside down, skid marks, and spilled oil. An officer was standing next to my car with Casey. The cop had a notepad out and was writing while Casey talked and shoved his fingers though his hair.

"That's your car there?" The cop next to me gestured at my car.

"Yeah."

"Okay, let's go over there and we can take your statement. First, though, are you okay? Do you need medical attention?"

"No, I'm fine. Just really shaken up, that's all."

We walked by Leo, now surrounded by EMTs and police officers.

"That's the passenger from—"

The CHP officer cut me off.

"Yes, we know. It's okay."

"It's not. It's not okay."

"Are you sure you don't need to get checked out, that you weren't hurt?"

"I'm fine."

We reached the car as Casey was rattling off his cell phone number for the officer with the notepad.

"I'm going to need your driver's license and a phone number where we can reach you," the cop holding my elbow said, smiling.

I opened my driver's side door while reciting my phone number for him and then plopped into the seat with my feet still out in the oily dirt. I closed my eyes for a moment and just listened to the sirens and tried to get the image of that dead guy out of my head, the sounds of that woman screaming out of my mind.

The other cop had a notebook out now and was leaning against my open car door. I felt a little like I was in trouble, which was stupid. I leaned back and reached behind the passenger seat for my purse. I was having trouble fishing my wallet out and realized my hands were shaking. I took a deep breath and produced the license from my bag. I handed it up to the patrolman and then leaned my shoulder back on the seat.

"Why don't we step over here for a moment so that Officer Creel can take your friend's statement," my officer said as he led me toward the side of the road. I looked back as Officer Creel took Casey to a cruiser and then I looked back at the cop next to me. I read his nametag. Officer Bacon. Oh, the poor guy. Why not just change your name? I almost chuckled but then the image of the passenger and Maureen's bloody teeth took over my head once again.

We stood in the tan dirt that kept the asphalt from the stretches of ice plant that kept us all from the sea. We were away from the chatter of the police radios and the screeches of creaking metal coming from the firemen trying to pry the door open on the sedan. We both faced out toward the ocean, toward the tiny white caps and the gulls and the fuzzy horizon. All I saw was that guy's bare feet in the brush and his dead eyes.

That woman, Maureen, just wanted more time. More time with Leo, more time being happy, more time on earth. I had all the time in the world, or thought I did. Maureen and Leo were just happy to *be*, they were all blank tape and possibility, now reduced to blood and glass and irremediable pain. My dad—my dad was blank tape and possibility, and he was cut down. What could he have done that I'll never know or appreciate? Here I had been, so focused on how Dad's death affected me or mom. What about Dad? I felt like everything, all the sudden assurance and comfort I had just held, was deflating around me.

I walked to my car. I still couldn't stop thinking about the dead guy. His eyes. Casey opened the passenger door and got in. He exhaled slowly and clicked his seatbelt into place. The officer stuck his head in my window.

"Okay, then. Like I said, we'll get that engine to move a little and you can be on your way."

He patted the hood of my car and nodded.

"Yeah, thanks."

"Oh, uh, I hope it's okay to ask you this, but you wouldn't happen to be Tommy Jasper's daughter, would you?"

Bacon looked down into the car at me, his eyebrows raised. I just looked back.

"It's just the LA address and the car and the name, and I have to say, you really do look a lot like him."

I nodded and smiled. I heard Casey make a sound that my mom always called "kissing teeth." *Don't you kiss your teeth at me, young lady*. Sort of a *tsk* sound on the inhale.

"Oh, wow. Listen, I am really sorry to hear about your dad passing away. I really loved his music. It meant a lot to me over the years, you know? Well, it's good to meet you."

"Good to meet you too. Thanks, uh, for your help today."

"No problem at all, Ms. Jasper. You drive safe now."

I waited a little while until the fire engine, its lights still swirling but no siren to be heard, eased into the dirt on the side of the road a bit to let me pass. I slowly crept along past the line of cars snaking down the road and stuck in traffic for what seemed to be miles. Casey didn't say anything and I didn't either. We were just quiet, my hands in a small tremble on the wheel. I could see drivers in the cars waiting to go north staring at us as we passed, the only car coming through from where the accident was. All those people, sitting there on the highway. They would be there for a while—that, I knew. We drove along, no sound. We came to the next exit and got off the highway in Goleta.

I pulled the car into a supermarket parking lot, cut the engine, and sat in silence. Casey gave a loud exhale and looked at me.

"Holy shit, huh?"

My hands still wouldn't stop shaking. I stared ahead, out at the steel jumble of shopping carts in the parking spot in front of me. The sun reflected off the cagework of metal and into my eyes, but I couldn't look away.

"That could have been us."

"I know, but it wasn't."

"But it could have been."

"Fuck, Clem, it *wasn't*. We're fucking alive. We lived. That's good."

"Yeah, I guess."

"You are a fucking good driver, that's for sure. That guy in the flipped car couldn't believe he didn't hit us."

"The lady in the convertible kept telling me there wasn't enough time. '*No, there's not enough time!*' That's what she kept yelling."

"Shit, dude, she's right."

"Sure."

I guess Casey didn't know what to say to that, since he just sat there looking out the window. After a while, he turned to me.

"What was up with that cop? Asking about your dad? What a fucking asshole."

"He wasn't an asshole. He was just curious. Whatever."

"Yeah, but there was some dude all dead on the side of the road and he's asking about your dad. I just thought it was gross."

"He has to be able to detach himself, you know? He can't dwell on all the fucked-up shit he sees all day."

"Yeah, well, his timing fucking sucks."

"My dad made him happy. My dad meant something to him. And my dad isn't around to thank him, so I will. What do you care, anyway?"

"I don't really."

We sat there some more, quiet and looking off in opposite directions. I didn't know what to think or feel. Relief, I guess. But there was something else.

"I'm going to make sure the roses didn't break."

I got out of the car and opened the trunk. The box was right where it was before. I opened the top and stared down at the lumps of bubble wrap. The roses were okay. But I wasn't. I was sobbing. I felt a hand on my shoulder and looked up to see Casey. An old man strolled by us, pushing his cart full of groceries toward his car. He glanced over at me and quickly looked away when he saw the state I was in. I felt a little bad for embarrassing him but just cried even harder.

"Clem, it's okay."

"What the hell is wrong with me? Why does everything have to be like this?" My voice got caught in my sobs.

"What do you mean?"

I cleared my throat, sniffled loudly, and looked up at him.

"I mean, why does everything have to be so hard? People die and people get hurt and nothing makes sense and everything is just shit."

"You're just shaken up from the accident."

"No. My dad is fucking dead. He's gone. But then I have to go on this trip and he's trying to teach me all this stuff about seeing the good things and feeling complete or whatever. And I thought for a little bit that I actually had that. But it's like I just saw clearly how selfish I am and how he's fucking dead and never coming back, and everything is horrible."

Casey stood up straight and put his hands on his hips. He exhaled slowly and looked out at the rest of the parking lot.

"You know what, Clem? I know you're sad about losing your dad. And I know that the trip has been stressful for you. But here you are, leaning against your $80,000 car, complaining about letters from a father who loved you more than anything, thinking about how shitty it's going to be to go back to your nice house and your full bank account and your supportive friends and family. You are sitting here in perfect health, with anything in the world available to you, saying that everything is horrible. That's not right, and it's not true. Open your fucking eyes. You have it all."

"I'm sorry." I felt like shit.

"Don't be sorry. Just see what you have. It's not just money. You have everything. Use it."

"I'm not an asshole, you know."

"I didn't say that."

"I'm just lost."

"Well, then you better get found. Because you can't go through life like this. Remember how you said you were happy to just *be*? Find that place again."

Casey turned and walked off, headed toward the coffee shop tacked on at the corner of the grocery complex. I got back in the driver's seat and stared at the parking lot, at the trees ringing the pavement, at the windshields reflecting the sun. I called the phone at my parents' place but no one answered, so I tried Mom's mobile. Again, all rings and no answer. I heard the sweet sound of her voice on the outgoing greeting and left a message.

"Hi Ma, it's Clem. I'm okay. Just, uh, call me when you get a chance."

I sat silently in the car and watched people come and go from the grocery store. Moms buying for their families, people on a break from work, the occasional lone senior.

There wasn't enough time. And I did need to recognize how good life was *right then*. I was alive. I was loved. I was healthy. I was aware. I reached into my purse and dug through my dad's letters. I flipped through each of them, reading his words and willing myself to see everything the way he did. If happiness was an inside job, I'd have to get fucking cracking.

The passenger door opened, and Casey got in the car. It looked like he'd splashed some water on his face and tried to pull himself together. Something I should have tried, too.

"You wanna go?" I asked.

"Sure."

I started the car and pulled out of the parking lot, making our way back to the freeway. When I saw the mileage sign announcing that Los Angeles was just one hundred and three miles away, I let out an enormous sigh. I could do one hundred and three miles, easy.

"We good?" Casey asked me.

"We're good."

I looked over at him and he smiled. I think what just happened was what Dena would call a refocus.

CHAPTER TWELVE

LOS ANGELES

"Death is the golden key that opens the palace of eternity."
—John Milton

The closer we got to LA, the more familiar everything looked, until finally we were in the LA basin. There was a dried yellow and brown background and the closer we got to home, the more billboards and grey buildings and tile roofs and palm trees and cars got piled on, until things were back to normal.

As I could have predicted, Casey lived in Echo Park. We got off the 101 at Alvarado Street and he directed me to his house. Casey reached around to the backseat and grabbed his messenger bag, pulling it into his lap. As he unbuckled his seatbelt, he looked over at me and smiled.

"Well, it's been interesting. Thanks again for letting me tag along with you."

I just smiled and looked down at my lap. Casey reached over and put his hand on my back.

"You'll be just fine, Clem. You'll find everything you need. And if you don't, it'll find you."

"Thanks."

"You can call me some time if you want. Or not."

"I think I might, Casey. You're a good guy."

"Sometimes."

With that, he got out of the car, walked up the path to his apartment building, and disappeared inside.

* * * * *

Traffic was a mess since it was getting dark and everyone just wanted to get home. I fought my way back up the 101 and then down Sunset toward my parents' place, my mom's house. I pulled into the drive just like I did on the day that Dad died. The only uncertainty I'd felt then was when I wondered if he would be okay. That's a yes or no question. The answer, of course, was no. But there was an answer all the same. As I parked the car, I knew I didn't have any yes or no questions left. And that was okay with me.

I took the box from the trunk and started toward the front door. Before I could get there, the door swung open and there was my mom, arms outstretched. I set the box at my feet and hugged her like I'd been gone for years instead of only five days. We went in the house and I told her about San Francisco and the drive down and the accident and my little breakdown in Goleta.

"Sounds to me like you've been overloaded in the last couple of days. That's a lot to experience and a lot of emotion. Especially for someone like you."

"What do you mean, someone like me?"

Mom put her arm around me.

"Oh, you know as well as anyone that you aren't the most . . ." she paused, ". . . *demonstrative* person. You're just not the expressive type. And that's okay. But you've been put through the wringer this week and I think you handled it very well."

Well, I wasn't sure about that. But I did feel pretty wrung out.

"So, what's in the box?"

Mom stared at the box of roses atop a table in the corner of the living room.

"That, my mama, is for you. I'm going to head home and take a shower, wash my clothes, and all that. You open it up, and I'll talk to you later."

I gave her another hug and a quick peck on the cheek and left. I couldn't bear to be there when she opened it. And I thought she'd need some time to herself. Time with just her and Dad.

* * * * *

Back at my house, I found that Sunny hadn't taken the mail in for the last couple of days, maybe the whole time I was gone. She did, however, leave a half-empty can of Sprite on the counter and a note telling me that everything was great and she was glad I would be back soon. I went out back and turned the hose on to water the jasmine. It was that time of day when the setting sun makes everything west-facing turn pink. The trunk of my neighbor's tree was cast in a rosy glow and I could hear some kids laughing in the street. I sighed and turned the water off, headed inside, and put my clothes in the wash.

After showering and making some tea, I sat on the sofa with Dad's last letter. I held it there in my lap for a while. Opening this one was going to be heavy. While there was the very good chance that it would explain exactly why I had to drive up and down the state, it was also the last new thing I would hear from him. Ever. It didn't really matter what he said in the letter, because as soon as I finished reading the thing, that was it. Keeping it sealed wouldn't do me any good, though. I'd have to open it some time and I did want to complete this task of his. I wanted it to come full circle. For a fleeting instant, I thought that maybe I would open the letter and he would be okay, he would be alive, and none of this would have ever happened. But as soon as I caught my index finger under the flap and started to tear, I knew that was just too good to be true. This letter, these thin pieces of paper in my hand, was all I had left.

Dear sweet Clem,

If you're a good girl, which I know you are, you are back in Los Angeles reading this letter. I really hope you didn't get all sneaky on me and open them all at once. That would suck to infinity. I crafted quite a little journey for you, my young one, and I hope you enjoyed it. I sure had a hell of a time putting it together. It was a real kick and sometimes a mind fuck, but for sure it was worth it. Come to think of it, these letters were probably the coolest thing anyone has ever willed to anyone else. That's monumental, if you ask me. Ha ha ha. Maybe I'll make the record books somewhere, the annals of dead guy history. Maybe not.

Where was I? Oh yeah, you're back in LA right now. You've driven up the state (well, not all the way up. I did cut you some mileage slack there) and back down again. I trust that you didn't get hurt or hurt anybody else and that you obeyed the rules of the road. I came up with a pretty good set of rules in all my years hauling over the pavement that crisscrosses this green planet. I had a separate set of rules for some places in Europe. In some of those countries, they all drive around in little scooter cars like ants in a newly garden-hosed hill. Whatever, we're talking the Good Ol' USA right now. Here are my (domestic) rules of the road (I should have told you these earlier, but I think you already know them):

Always stop for pedestrians

If you leave a burger wrapper in the car, you'll regret it the next day

If you see something cool, pull over and check it out

Click it or ticket (ha ha ha, I love that one. Seatbelts are important.)

If you can choose, always pick open windows over air conditioning

I bet you have a whole set of your own now. Everyone's got to put their own scheme together, you know? Did you know that Jerry has this thing where he has to stop at every truck stop diner he sees, just to pick up a matchbook? Every couple of years he rides his motorcycle across the country, so that's a lot of diners and a lot of fucking matches. He'll usually sample the fare there too, but even if he's not hungry, he still has to stop and get a damned matchbook. He's got boxes of them all over his house. That's probably not safe, keeping cardboard boxes of matchbooks around the house. I'll have to tell him to get some metal bins or something. Or maybe keep them in one of those fireproof safes? But I think that's just to keep fire out, not in. I don't know.

But back to Los Angeles. I keep getting sidetracked, sweet thing. Sorry about that. Anyway, I wanted you to come full circle. To start in LA and wind up here too. Los Angeles is a real mind-shatterer, both in a good way and a bad. It's a place that can shut you out if you let it. And it's a place that can crush a person. But it's also the only city I know where dreams just explode out of every mind and hill and ocean wave. Think of all the great things that were figured out right here and all the great artistic minds that have come here to make their ideas and dreams into something they can share with everybody in the world. You can show up here as one thing and remake yourself into anything you want. That's America, baby! The weather is perfect, the smog gives us kick-ass sunsets, and we have the best basketball team on the planet. Ah, the Lakers. Don't get me started on those guys. But what I am trying to say is that Los Angeles is home.

I know I wasn't the average dad. I know that a lot of the time I was away and that was hard for you and Dena and Simon. But I had a calling and I had to make a living the only way I knew how. I did the very best to provide for the family and protect you three from the ills of the world, and I think I did a damned good job. In your case, maybe too good of a job. You've never known anything bad, so I wonder if that's what makes it hard for you to know anything really good. You have the capability to feel great emotion, I know that. But I think that sometimes you don't know that. That's not the point right now, though. What I am trying to tell you is that we have kind of an eccentric family. I wasn't the guy coming home at five o'clock and mowing the lawn on the weekends. I wasn't the dude coaching soccer or showing you guys how to ride bikes. But I think that I made up for that in other ways. After all, you were the kids who went all over the world and hung out backstage at British rock festivals. You brought the harmonica Springsteen gave you for show-and-tell one year. You were the kids who inspired me to write things that inspired people all across this planet. That's pretty wild, isn't it?

You've played a part in everything that I've done from the very moment you popped out of your mama and into this world. For that, my little love, I thank you. Really, I thank you from the very bottom of my goofy old heart. You and Dena and Simon and your mother have blessed me more than I could have ever imagined. You guys are me. Without you all, I just don't exist. I was nothing, not worthy of anything at all. Then I created the blank slate of a man that each of you has colored into someone I think is pretty fucking fantastic. Is that egotistical? I don't really care. Ha ha ha. All I know is that my family is everything to me. I see Los Angeles as both the birthplace of my family and a representation of family itself. The gift I tried to give to you (the gift that I never had until I had you guys) was a place to come back to. A place to know where you'll always be loved and safe and protected. It's not LA or the house or any place physically specific. It's your brother and your sister and your mother. And since I must be gone if you're reading this letter, you still have me too. I am with you forever. Even if you aren't home, I will always be with you, and that is home enough.

This isn't over yet, my Clemetine. There's one more stop for you. One more thing to understand, one more thing to make right. I bet you thought this was it, because this was the last letter you got, but not so! In the envelope with this letter is a key. It's to a safety deposit box at a big bank full of people in suits who were surprisingly nice to me. Ha ha ha. The address and the box number are on the tag attached to the key. Everything in the box is for you and you alone. I am serious about the alone part. Your eyes only. It's the final piece, the missing link, the explanation, the meaning of life. Well, maybe not the meaning of life. But it is something I've needed to explain and just couldn't. Something I needed to finish and wasn't sure how.

Go check it out. I'll be there with you, of course. I always am.
Lovey love love,
Dad

I couldn't believe it. I tipped the envelope to the side and watched the tiny key slide out and into my palm. A fucking safe deposit box? I didn't really have the energy to feel any sort of dread or anxiety about it. The answer to all this, to the trip and the mystery and, I guess, Dad's life, was in that box. I looked at the clock, 9:24 p.m. Too late to go to the bank. I held the key on my hand, turning it over and feeling the box number engraved on the side.

I got up, went into my bedroom, and slammed the key onto the top of my dresser. This was torture, plain and simple. What the hell had I done to deserve this; the endless highs and lows and every bit of being unsure in-between? What if I got to the box and there was another letter, another ten letters, another key? What if this never ended? At what point would I feel like I was done, if ever? And would it ever make me stop missing my dad?

I knew it wouldn't. Nothing was ever going to make that part of me whole again. Everyone loses their parents at some point, I told myself. Shit, my dad never had them to begin with, really. So why couldn't I pull myself together? I was mad at Dad for the whole ridiculous trip, for not being direct, for dying when I really needed him. I was mad at myself for not realizing I needed him when I had him and for being such a passive waste of space. I was mad at . . . shit, I was just mad. Mad at everything.

I stretched out on the bed and stared at the ceiling. I could hear the contained thumping of a car stereo on full blast in a car with its windows up as it rolled down my street. Someone going somewhere, doing something. The vibrations of the bass set off a car alarm farther down the block, the series of trills and squawks going unanswered for what felt like an eternity until it shut itself off with three short beeps. A safe deposit box. The more I thought about it, the more ridiculous it seemed. I started thinking about how bizarre this whole plan was to begin with and how perfectly fitting it was. Dad could be sort of a spacey mess sometimes and that's exactly what this scavenger hunt through his history had become. I was sure he saw himself as some groovy cosmic agent, stalling his own demise with fringed suede cloak and dagger. This was Dad not going anywhere.

I started laughing at the absurdity of it all. Sure, he told me some seriously heavy stuff, but in the end, it was all kind of a joke. I was the one who made it into something with *gravitas*. Well, Mom did too. Just as we each saw Dad as the person we thought he should be or that we wanted him to be, the whole trip and all the letters were our own constructs. It was like Casey said. Perception. We put our spin on it and never looked back. Never looked directly at it. That was the lesson, I guessed.

The phone rang and I reached over to the bedside table to grab it.

"Hi, honey."

"Hey, Ma."

"Those roses, Clem . . ."

She trailed off and I couldn't think of anything to say to fill the space. We sat quietly for a little bit, holding phones to our ears across town. Finally, I said something.

"I know," was all I could muster.

"I feel guilty for doubting him, but then these remind me that he loved me, no matter what."

"He really did love you, Mom. He loved all of us more than we ever understood."

"He still loves us, baby girl."

I chuckled.

"You're right. He's still here, that's for sure."

"So what's next, Clem? Did this crazy trip give you any insight?"

"Into what, Dad?"

"Dad, you, life, your future . . . anything."

"I'm still processing a lot of it but I feel like something has changed. I feel like I'm at the beginning of understanding things."

"I know, hon, and you'll figure things out in your own time. But I think that this is a good opportunity to make some changes, figure out what you want to do."

"I guess so. Dad talked about starting fresh, being a blank tape. I guess that's me now."

"Well, you just have to find yourself, you know. Find out who you are, and then you can start being that person. That's growing up."

CHAPTER 13

"Three things cannot be long hidden: the sun, the moon, and the truth."

—Buddha

The next morning I spent a good half hour sitting in my car on Wilshire Boulevard in front of the bank, waiting for it to open. At ten to nine, the nervous energy was too much for me, so I got out and stood outside, patting my pocket to be sure the key hadn't fallen out. It was already a little warm, that smog layer still hanging on, holding everything in. I shielded my eyes from the sun reflecting off the front doors while listening to people's flip flops clap up and down the sidewalk, the occasional snippet of a phone conversation, car alarms blipping in and out of activation. My phone blipped and I saw that it was a text from Simon: *Ma said you were back. Everything cool?* I quickly typed back: *Everything is cool and I love you, sweet brother.* A few seconds later came his reply: *Love you, too, sis.* I smiled. I thought he'd make fun of me, not take my sentiment seriously. I guess things were changing. At last, a security guard came over and unlocked the door, letting me in to the lobby with its marble and harsh lighting and desks arranged on maroon carpeting. I walked toward the back and asked to access my safe deposit box, showed some young guy in a suit my key, and signed a logbook. My heart was pounding and I was starting to sweat around my temples. I hoped the guy didn't think I was up to no good. This was it. This was the last of it, the end of this adventure. The suit led me into the vault of boxes and I unlocked the box, my hands shaking the whole time. He showed me to a room with a table and two chairs.

"Please, take your time. I'll be outside at the counter when you are ready or if you need any assistance."

I thanked him and waited until he closed the door, waited for the click of the handle. Then I slowly opened the box.

There were old photos, some newspaper clippings, a few papers, and an envelope. I slowly started removing each piece, looking them over, trying to understand.

The photos were all of my family throughout the years, except for one. It was an old black and white, the kind with that quarter-inch border of white all the way around. It was of a little boy on the bank of a river. He had sandy blond hair and a black eye. It was my father. I turned the photo over and written on the back in pencil was just "Age 8." I didn't recognize the handwriting. I flipped it back over and looked at my dad. Filthy clothes and a gapped smile and that glint in his eye, that bruised-up eye. This was the only thing I'd ever seen that actually connected Dad to that time, to his childhood. I'd either never asked or been told vague nothings about his early years. Now he was staring me in the face and I felt shamed for not wanting to know more, sooner. I stared at the picture a while longer, trying to absorb every detail. Then I set it aside and pulled out the newspaper clippings.

There were two time-yellowed stories from the *Stockton Record*. The first was headlined, "Man Found Dead off Pacific Avenue." It said a guy was found dead from an apparent blow to the head, that his identity couldn't be disclosed until his next of kin was informed, that police suspected he'd been a patron at one of the nearby taverns and asked anyone who had any information to contact them. I read the story over and over. I didn't know what this had to do with anything but figured it couldn't be good. I picked up the other article.

"No Leads in Death of Drifter" was the other headline. I started to read the article and then stopped. I started to read it again but all the words were jumbling together. I was feeling a dizzy and had to set the clip down on the table. I looked up at the ceiling. This was not fucking happening.

. . . authorities have been unable to locate any relatives of the man, who has since been identified as Thomas Jasper of no fixed address in Stockton. Those familiar with Jasper at local bars and drinking establishments said Jasper kept to himself and spoke once of being raised in an orphanage. The medical examiner has ruled Jasper's death accidental, stating that Jasper died after

striking his head on the sidewalk as a result of falling while intoxicated.

I opened the envelope.

* * * * *

Dear Clem,

Mind fuck of the highest order. I am afraid that's what I have handed you. I am sorry about that. This is how it had to be though, my little cosmic traveler. I made a decision long ago and that choice put my whole life in a direction. As that direction started picking up people and creating people and creating a livelihood for me and everyone I'd involved, well . . . there was no going back, no explaining, no need to ruin a good thing. I still had the need to share my truth with someone. You, sunshine love, are that someone. What you decide to do with that truth, with that notion of me—that's up to you. You are a strong girl; my little squirrel with the heart of a bear. You and me, we both tumble through life. This is just part of your tumble now.

So here's what happened. I ran away from home. I got tired of getting the shit knocked out of me every single day. Punch in the gut, punch in the soul, it was all the same. I was getting destroyed and I left. I went to Stockton first. I meant to get to San Francisco and I eventually did. But I took a baby step first and headed to Stockton.

Stockton back then was a shipping town. I don't know what it's like now. Probably subdivisions and minivans, ahoy! But back then, it was all train tracks and shipping channels and trucks and people from all over. I wasn't there long—like, two weeks—but it was a good primer for San Francisco. I met people from almost every corner of the world in Stockton. Good people.

I stayed at the YMCA, right in the middle of downtown, and not far from that famous Deep Water Channel. I was gathering myself. Getting myself together. I was young, so I also got into a bit of bad business. There were some shady bars near the channel that would serve just about anybody, even a smooth-faced kid like me. Here's the thing—I knew what I didn't want to be. I didn't want to be a migrant picker who hated everyone around him. I didn't want to be a man who would bring sorrow to his own flesh and blood. But the only things I really knew at that point in my life, other than music's sneaking whisper, were the bottle and the fist. For that brief time, I became what I tried to run away from.

I was insecure, we'd say now. I wanted to prove myself. And the only way I'd been shown how to deal with the world was in an angry, boozy haze.

So I poked around the bars, became just another soul drifting in and out of the scene. I got sauced, ran my mouth, wandered back to my room. Rinse, repeat.

Clem, this is the hardest fucking thing I've ever done. I've kept this locked up in me and never let it out. Understand that for me to share this with you . . . well, that's just a testament to who I know you to be.

I got drunk at this place called Merchants. I was sitting there, adding a blur to the noise around me. Listening to stories, letting them bleed into me and into my story. A guy came up next to me. He had the room across from mine at the Y. He was all smiles—a real cheery drunk. A lot like Jerry. Goofy. He started talking about how he was going to get a job with the highway department, that he loved hard work. He wouldn't shut up, and he was just so fucking happy. About working for the highway department! He was getting on my nerves, but it wasn't a big thing. Until he said something that just flipped a switch inside of me.

See, when my old man was on a tear and was really laying into me, he used to say, "You're nothing but a little river rat, anyway. Just a dirty shit river rat." River rat was the lowest thing he could call you, but also his badge of honor. He was proud to be a piece of trash who lived on the river in nothing but poison negativity.

So when this guy called me that, said he and I were both just river rats, I lost it. I moved down to the other end of the bar and ordered another cheap shot of whiskey. The guy just scooted down and ordered the same, still talking about the highway department and an honest day's work. I thought I could tune him out but then he started in with that river rat shit again. I got up, shoved by him, and stormed out of the bar. The damn fool followed me, though. Followed me with this huge grin, saying, "Hey brother, I'm just saying we're the same! Us river rats gotta stick together!"

He followed me down a few empty blocks, blathering on about workers and sweat and damned river rats. I just couldn't take it anymore.I turned around and grabbed him by his grubby work shirt, unable to say anything at all with so much rage running all through me. Rage about every microscopic part of my being, you know? I stared at him and his eyes got huge but he never stopped smiling. So I shoved him as hard as I could. He fell back, hit his head on the curb. Didn't move. I stood there on the street, no one around, listening to my own breathing and looking at this poor guy, his eyes open and rolled back in his head. He had a religious medal on a chain around his neck that had snapped off in my hand when I grabbed him. The chain and the medal, St. Anthony, dangled from my fingers and I felt the lowest anyone could feel. This poor guy was nothing but amity. He was happy and filled with starlight optimism and I snuffed it out, just like that. I was my father, and it made me sick. I looked around and didn't see a soul, so I went back to my room at the Y and had the craziest drug-free trip ever known. I spaced out, sitting there seeing myself as my old man, as a rotted shell of cosmic crap. I gripped that medal tight and I saw the man I'd killed with that smile on his face and his excitement about everything around him. That St. Anthony medal was the only thing left of him, the only piece of the real him on earth. I destroyed a man, a living creature, a spirit, a SOUL, and I needed to make up for it.

I laid low for a while and figured out what to do. I found out they said it was an accident, the guy dying. Chalked it up to some drunk falling over after going on a bender. Some cops asked me about what happened, what with me staying across the hall from him and all. I told them I didn't know a thing but that he was my friend. They didn't seem to give a shit, anyway. Turned out he didn't have any next-of-kin; he was an orphan or something. The people running the Y put his clothes in a box for needy guys passing though. I poked into his room and found his birth certificate wedged under the mattress, so I grabbed it. I wasn't sure why at the time. I heard that some Catholic Women's group paid to have him cremated and they spread his ashes in the Sacramento River. I wondered how they knew that's what he probably would have wanted. I guess some things are just so right they can't help but be.

I can't believe I am telling all this to you. I am scared shitless, but it feels kind of good to actually put this down somewhere outside of my head.

Anyway, I made a promise to the old me and to Tommy Jasper that I would make a change. I traded places with him. I had this intense feeling that I had absorbed his energy and rid myself of the me I'd been burdened with. I would carry on for him and do great things, all in his name. I mean, I didn't go work for the highway department because, let's face it, I am just not cut out for that kind of thing. I thought he'd understand. And every time I roll the roads in this world, spreading love and music to everyone I can, I think that's part of the dream he had, I had. Our dream.

I'll never make up for what I did. I can't. But I spend every single moment of every single day trying to be better. Trying to put some balance to the horrible thing I did. Was I a coward? Maybe. But there are all kinds of justice in this world, my baby. You'll see that. I'm just trying to make things right.

So what do I want you to do with all this? Take a deep breath, first. Be pissed off, be sad, be ashamed, be understanding, be whatever you like. I just want you to know. I want you to find the real me, not some name or anything but my actual soul. Know that what I've done doesn't erase the love I have for you, your mother, your brother and sister, for everyone in the human race. If anything, what I did clarified that love.

This is everything you need to know. You are reading this, so you've lost me. But now you found me, baby girl. That's it. You found me. This is me, a separate entity from you. You know the "why" of my journey now. Now, go find your "why." Just don't let it ever be borne of desperation or a need for redemption. Let it come from your pure, beautiful heart. That's my gift to you.

I love you, my Clementine.

I tipped the envelope to the side and a small silver pendant and chain slid out and onto the tabletop. The St. Anthony medal. I held it in my shaking hands and read the letter again. So many things made sense; things my Dad said or believed over the years, that subliminal pain he tried to hide that I now realized painted all of us for all this time. I fastened the chain around my neck and couldn't believe how at peace I felt. Here I'd thought that the big bad reveal would be a sordid affair. That was the worst I could imagine. My father had killed a man and I finally felt calm.

* * * * *

I put the contents of the box in a big envelope provided by the bank and slipped it into my purse.

As I walked out to my car, the sun had chased away the smog and the day was bright, putting everything in sharp focus. St. Anthony, the medal around my neck felt heavy, but in a secure way. It was all so much to take in but that sense of dread and anxiety that had followed me since I opened the first letter dissolved like that morning's cruddy air. I knew it all now. No secrets. And this knowledge was like a key, decoding the rest of my dad's experiences and my life too.

I drove home and kept thinking about St. Anthony. I didn't know anything about saints or medals or religion. But the name St. Anthony kept tickling at the back of my mind. I'd heard it before, I knew it. I got home and headed right for my old collection of records. Flipping past Duran Duran and The Police and Vanity 6 and Guns N' Roses, I found what I was looking for. *Bathtub Epiphany*. Dad's clunker of a solo album.

I sat on the floor with that ridiculous record in my hands. The cover art was some weird, spectral, cosmic painting I suppose was meant to alert the listener that minds were about to be blown. Streaks of light and stars and what looked to be ribbons floated out from a crayon drawing of an eyeball in the center of the piece. Oh, Dad. I know what you were trying to do.

I slid the record out and scanned the liner notes on the sleeve. There it was. The last song on the album. This was a particularly difficult subject for Dad—this album in general, but also this last song. Most of the reviews (all of which panned the shit out of the album) really tore the last song to shreds. It was just Dad and an acoustic guitar at the core. But then he'd overlaid the whole thing with hackneyed psychedelic effects like echo boxes and digital who-knows-whats, and the result was a muddled and strange swing and a miss. I remember Dad wouldn't get off the couch one day because the review in *Rolling Stone* called the whole album "laughable" and the last track "painfully muddled and unoriginal" and "a joke that's only funny to Jasper." He just curled up under a blanket and wouldn't talk to any of us.

I looked at the lyrics for the song and the key turned in yet another lock.

"The Blistered Shove of Memory"
Every road I travel
Every truth and shout
I start all over
To know what it's all about
The gray flannel night
When loss and love combined
It was early and late
It was wrong and right
I'm the son of the four winds
The oily rain in the gutter
I'm St. Anthony's crying nightfall
The bastard child of no mother
I know you want to be like me, baby
But make your own bad choices
Those quiet voices
With you wherever you go
Those reminders of missteps and casualties
I'm the quiet voice now—that's me
Old as the grit in your boot
New as the crack in your window pane
That's the blistered shove of memory
You, me, him, her, all the same
Give me your life, I'll give you mine

Give me your life, I'll give you mine
Give me your life, I'll give you mine

Holy shit. The world thought this song was just a clumsy piece of mid-tempo studio mess. But it was Dad's heart, his confession to them.

All this information provided some sort of closure and understanding but it was a hell of a burden. I don't know how he kept it all to himself for so long. I guess he had to. I had the urge, though, to tell someone. To talk about it. I felt like I couldn't fully process or appreciate everything—Dad's secret, the trip, my role in all of this—until I talked about it. I was always the one listening, always the one absorbing. Now I needed to share.

There was just no way I could tell Mom. She'd been through enough and I didn't want to tarnish the memories she had. Her worst fear was infidelity, not accidental manslaughter. I couldn't tell Simon or Dena either. Dena made everything a mission. She wouldn't be able to just let this be. She would feel compelled to do something, even though there's nothing to be done. Simon would be more concerned with how this impacted him. Sunny was too much of a flake and just wouldn't get it. I felt like maybe Casey would understand this, but then I remembered how little I really knew about him, how easily he could leak the story if he wanted to, and how Dad had said this part was just for me. My eyes only. The one person I could talk to about this was gone. All I had left were memories and letters. And I guess that's all I had to give too.

I went to my desk and got out a notebook. I'm not sure why I bought it in the first place, I think I liked the flower design on the cover, all blues and greens and subtly happy. I'd never used it, never written anything in its pages. I sat down and started to write.

Dear Dad,

So this is what it's like to feel. To really feel things. The intensity of all this has been too much at times but I am starting to think that too much is exactly what I needed.

I thought losing you was the start of everything crumbling. But now I know two things. First, I didn't lose you. Truth is, I found you. And the other thing is that everything is always crumbling, always changing, and I guess that's okay. That's living life. That's what it is like to be and to enjoy it.

I was so scared when I first went on the trip. I thought that maybe you wanted to introduce me to some secret family. Or that you'd been in love with someone other than Mom and that maybe you weren't the true and honest guy I knew as my dad. So it's kind of weird to find out that, yeah, you had this crazy secret and that it was that you accidentally killed someone. What's weirder and crazier is that I don't seem to have too much trouble getting my head around this.

I know you carried a lot of guilt with you all those years and did everything you could to try and redeem a situation that just couldn't be repaired. You couldn't bring that guy back, so you swapped with him, I guess we'd say. I think—wait, I KNOW—you did the best you could and that you made some sort of cosmic amends for everything. God, see? I read enough of your letters and I start talking like you. Cosmic? You are probably laughing right now. I like to think that you are always just over my shoulder. That you are watching me, and I hope you are pleased.

I know now that you can't go through life not feeling. Because that just isn't life. Life is the tastes and the smells and the sounds, but it's also the bruises and the smiles and the giggles and the moans and the stings and the overwhelming joy and the deepest, chest-smashing despair. Can't have one extreme without the other, and without either, there's just nothing at all. You've taught me so much in these last few weeks and I know that these are things you'd tried to teach me my whole life. I guess now is just the time when I'm ready. It was supposed to be now.

So let's talk a little about your bombshell, Dad. Holy fucking shit. At first I thought that I had no idea who you really were. But that only flashed in my head for a minute. I immediately realized that I just didn't know your original name. (See, I didn't even say real *name. Is there such a thing?). You must have been that Martin kid that Lee mentioned. Yup, I met your friend Lee in Walnut Grove. At least I think it was him. I was still too scared then to face things head on and I had no idea this whole other identity thing was even on the table. You would have to admit that it's an insane story. Death, assumed identities. How is it that no one figured this out before? How did you keep it such a secret?*

I always felt like you did the right thing, no matter what. While I am not sure if that's true or not anymore, I know that you always did what you felt to be the right thing. And that's the right thing for you. I mean, I guess we only know what we feel and all this time I was never really feeling anything, so how could I know anything? But you did what you thought was right and good. You made your version of amends. And you showed me who you really were. You were, are, and always will be a good man. And the most important part of that is that you were, are, and always will be just a man. Just a human being. A good one, yes, but still human. Being human means feeling, and it means making mistakes (and making beautiful things too). All that messiness is part of the process.

I realize now that every one of us has who we are and then who we are to other people. And every person we meet or know gets their own version. I feel like now, though, I have a better idea of who you were to yourself. That's a pretty major gift to give to someone and I thank you forever for it.

So we leave this trail of messy victories and defeats, and that trail is just a series of memories. It's like an oil slick, where every angle and perspective gives you a different color or sheen. Every person sees that slick differently. I guess we also get to choose how we see and remember those things. I am choosing to remember you as the best dad anyone could have known. I remember you as a man who loved his family more than anything and would do anything for them and protect them from the less wonderful parts of life. I remember you as a man who put everything into trying to give people brief moments of joy. And for the most part, you were very successful with that. Your music made a lot of people happy and that's a pretty huge accomplishment. I remember you as a guy who came from a sad and terrible beginning and worked to correct that. I remember you as a silly guy who loved to laugh and look at the sky and hug people and embrace the ridiculous things in life. These are my memories. Mine alone.

How do you remember me? I want you to know me as a daughter who loves her family, loves her father. Remember me as a daughter who is trying to do right. I want everyone I meet from this point forward to eventually remember me as someone who was present, connected, here.

I love you, Dad. And I want you to know that I am on the right track. Whatever that is. I am starting to enjoy the process of things. I am starting to really feel and I am liking that.

Thank you for showing me your life. Thank you for always being there and for being there still.

I miss you. I always will. But I know you are here. I don't need unopened letters to have you around. I don't even need letters I've read. I've got my memories and that's my truth. And in that truth, I've got you.

Love,

Clem

* * * * *

I took Olympic all the way down to the ocean and then headed north on PCH. It was a little hazy out but starting to clear up and the ocean was a gorgeous expanse. I opened the sunroof and let the salt air whip around me. Dena always talks about how ocean air is ionized and makes you feel energized or some shit. I was starting to believe her.

There was a good amount of traffic on the road and as I headed through Malibu Colony, I felt really confident about what I planned to do. The Pacific Coast Highway began to arch away from the water a bit and I knew I was almost there. I turned left and made my way through the streets of thick hedges and front gates toward the ocean and the cliff where I first said goodbye to my dad. I reached Cliffside Drive and there it was again. The dusty, sandy cliff and the Pacific Ocean beyond. The air here was cleaner than in LA, sweetened by sea breezes and well-tended landscaping.

I got out of the car, envelope in hand, and walked the path to the cliff's edge. I'd expected there to be other people out here, what with the great weather and all, but I was all alone. I sat down on the path, just like Jerry had done only a couple of weeks ago. Birds kited around on the air and I looked down at the water churning below and thought about the marigolds. A log, tossed and tumbled by the surf, was wedged on the rocks below. Driftwood. I smirked, reached into the envelope, and pulled out the news clippings. As I stared out at the water, I began pulling the yellowed paper into little bits, making a snowy pile in my cupped hands. I waited until the wind whipped around a little and when I was sure it was heading out to sea instead of back into my face, I held out my hands and let go. In a move like a cheap magician releasing his weary doves, I sent the scraps of my dad's greatest secret out to the ocean. The flakes of paper scattered up on the breeze and then drifted down into the Pacific. Gone with the marigolds and Dad.

Next, I took Dad's final letter out of the envelope. I read it again and pressed the St. Anthony medal against my chest. Dad felt he owed Tommy. Owed him a life, so he made his right. I didn't know if that was justice but it was what happened. The truth, I realized, is that we all owe everyone else our lives. We all owe it to each other to always make it right. It was then that I felt more connected to my father, to the entire world, to myself than ever before. I found that the best you can do is to always try to make it right, whatever your "it" is.

I ripped Dad's letter into little squares and let them go on the wind, one by one. His final message to me was swallowed by the ocean in tiny bites. When at last my hand was empty, I pulled my letter to Dad out of my pocket and opened it. Flattening the sheets of paper against my thighs, I smoothed my hands across my words to Dad. I thought about how wonderful it was to feel so very sad.

I tore the letter into strips and let it go into the wind and the ocean below. Dad did his best to make it right and that was between us. I found him and now I could let it go—for both our sakes. The pieces of my letter fluttered down like ribbons. I watched them land in the surf and disappear.

EPILOGUE

The tapping of rain on the roof woke me. I let out a huge sigh and rolled over onto my back. Out the window, splashes of rain plunked off the leaves of the jasmine bush. Everything was getting clean, getting washed up at last. Everything clean, everything moving. I stared up at the ceiling and smiled to myself. It was nice being still.

I still had one more day before I started working at Mar's bookstore. He'd started selling his used books online for super-cheap and he needed someone to manage and fulfill the orders that had come in at a volume far larger than he ever expected. I'd get to help out the occasional in-person customer as well. But I would be surrounded all day long by stories and that's what made me happy. I knew that my story was actually just everyone else's stories and absorbing those stories is what made me feel whole. Those stories filled my blank tape. That was tomorrow, though. There was still today and it seemed to be inhabited more and more by memories of my dad.

Dad loved days like this, when cool rain set the day in motion. He especially loved to go outside when the rain stopped. He loved how the pavement smelled as the rain began to evaporate into the air. He'd experienced this all over the world and never tired of it. *Take a deep breath*, he'd say. *Nice, huh?* The rain was still coming down, though, and I watched as it hit the window panes and listened as it tinkled down the gutters on the roof.

After a time I got up and crept to the kitchen, leaving the cream dollop warmth of the duvet. I poured myself a glass of cranberry juice and switched on the radio. I was watching the rain dissolve away into the day, slowly taper off into nothing, when I heard aloud the song that had been in my head for months. There, strumming out of the tiny gray speakers, was Dad. They were playing "Loving Rose." I looked back out the window and saw that the sun was starting to peek out from the blanket layer of clouds above. I put my hand to the St. Anthony medal around my neck and stared at the radio and tried to remember how Dad's face looked when he sang, wondered what went through his mind.

"You were there . . . it was me you chose . . . I'll hold you close . . . my Loving Rose . . . sun's in my eyes . . . everything gold . . . I'll make it all up to you . . . someday . . . she's a Loving Rose . . . I found myself a Loving Rose . . . tossed and tumbled, waiting to be found . . . so much of this wide world to see . . . and then that Loving Rose found me . . ."

My phone rang, and I looked down at the incoming number. Casey.

"Hey, you."

"Hey, Clem. I'm going to stop by the store before I come over. Need anything?"

"Me? Not a thing."

"Okay, see you in a little bit."

"Drive safe."

"I know, I know . . . no one knows how to drive in the rain. See you soon."

I went out to the driveway and stood between two puddles. The clouds moved further and further to the east, ceding more of the sky to the sun. I took a deep breath.

Everybody gets found eventually.

ACKNOWLEDGMENTS

Thanks to all who loved/guided/inspired/supported, especially:

Jennifer McCartney and all at Skyhorse; Willy Maley, Andrew Radford, Tom Leonard, Laura Marney, and all at the University of Glasgow Creative Writing program; Sharon Dutton; Travis Dutton; Frank Nemec; Laura Villasenor; Brady Baltezore; Aaron Gregoire; Bruce Bowman; Rebecca White Prevette; Heath Milligan, Max Everhart and all at Northeastern Technical College; the California Highway Patrol; Graham Douglas; Eliot.